The cr

ain.

I move d the
door a
listen. n't
known the
old hou

I started to close the door.

Just then Allen came from the kitchen. He passed through full moonlight on his hurried way to the front door.

I clasped my hand over my mouth to stifle the escaping sound of shock and watched frozen as the door shut and locked behind him.

What was Allen doing in our kitchen at two o'clock in the morning?

The broom closet. The door leading to the basement!

Available from Crosswinds

Frog Eyes Loves Pig
by James Deem

The Black Orchid
by Susan Rubin

Stu's Song
by Janice Harrell

The HOUSE with the IRON DOOR

Margaret Mary Jensen

CROSSWINDS

New York • Toronto
Sydney • Auckland
Manila

To five I love
Heather, Jennifer, James
Victoria and Anthony

First publication August 1988

ISBN 0-373-98029-9

Printed in the U.S.A.

RL 4.7, IL age 11 and up

MARGARET MARY JENSEN was born in Kentucky, the youngest of nine children in a family whose members took turns telling stories in the evenings. She sold her first story at age seven, to her brother for a quarter. Since then she has published four adult novels, a first-grade reader and more than forty short stories. The author currently lives in Los Angeles, California.

Chapter One

I stretched and discovered that my blouse had stuck to the back of the seat again. My mouth was sand dry, and my skin burned. A buzzard circled in the clear sky, and an eerie stillness hung in the air. Only the whirr of the Jeep's engine penetrated the silence.

Miles back, I had seen a sign, This Road Not Patrolled. What if we had car trouble? I was on the edge of being really scared. Neither my mom nor I knew anything about fixing a car. And there was nothing out here but sagebrush, cactus and distant purple mountains that looked no closer than they had an hour ago. That was when we had left the freeway and Mom let me drive. I guess she thought it would shut me up, but it hadn't.

I glanced at her. "I still don't see why we had to

come,'' I said. ''Anyway, I don't believe there is a town.''

Mom looked up from the California map she was studying. ''There's a town, April. It's just that the Mojave Desert is so big.'' Mom folded the map and watched the road again. Although I'd gotten my driver's license on my sixteenth birthday six months ago, she still looked worried when I drove. I knew her worry then had little to do with my driving.

I swerved to miss a large rock in the deep tire tracks I was following. ''What doctor would come way out here?'' I said.

''I'm a doctor. I've come out here, and so did your grandfather, and he was one of the best.''

''Too bad he never got to practice.''

''April, please. You'll love it.''

Mom thought being a teenager put you in the fast lane to happiness. ''Name one thing I'll like about this place,'' I said.

''You'll get a good tan. Now put your hat on.'' Mom had a basket of contradictions like this. How could I get a tan wearing a wide-brimmed hat?

Tan made me think of Jerry. Jerry really liked tall blond girls with great legs and a good tan. I met one of the requirements. I was tall. Oh, yes, I met another requirement I forgot to mention. I had a garage he could practice his drums in. But the few times Jerry kissed me, I forgot all about not being blond with great legs and a tan. Now it would be a whole summer before I saw Jerry again. Maybe I wouldn't be seeing him even then. He was already practicing someplace else. He started the day we began packing to leave Seattle for Sand Canyon.

"I just wish I had come sooner," Mom said, shattering my thoughts.

"How could you? You didn't know sooner," I told her.

"He was my father. I should have known something wasn't right from his last letter."

"I don't know when things aren't right for my father," I said.

Mom gave me an exasperated look. She hated it when I mentioned Dad. Dad is, or at least was, a musician, like Jerry. He left with a band when I was three, and he never came back. Mom used to say he was in Australia and that he would be sending for us soon. But all the time I was growing up, I never once saw a letter from there. Most of the time I tried not to think about him. But sometimes, like with Mom talking about her father, I naturally thought of mine.

Mom's hands gripped the edge of the seat at the same time she yelled, "Look out!"

The Jeep leaped into a dry wash and rocked and bounced across to the other side while I fought the wheel for control. When we were back in the tracks, she took a deep breath. "I think I should drive."

"No. I'll slow down. But when we get to this town of yours, I'm going to complain to the commissioner of roads."

We drove awhile with only the hum of the engine between us. When the surrounding feeling of desolate loneliness crept into the Jeep, I said, "Mom, I really wish you hadn't promised to come."

"I'll stay until that young man Dad helped through medical school returns and takes over." Her face grew sad. "I promised Dad that much in my last letter."

"What makes you think when this man becomes a doctor, he'll return?"

"Because Dad thought he would. He told me a lot about him in letters. He's due to arrive by the end of summer. We can sell him the house and equipment. The money can go in your college fund."

"I hope Grandpa was right," I said. "But maybe I won't go to college; instead I might be a model, or basketball player." I joked about my height, but I worried, too, that I hadn't stopped growing at five-eight.

"Your grandfather was a doctor, I'm a doctor and you will be a doctor," Mom said. "It's in your blood."

"Is that why I get sick at the sight of it?"

Mom laughed. "You'll get over that."

A jackrabbit bounded across the road in front of the Jeep. "Don't hit him," Mom cried.

"I'd never hit a patient of yours," I said. "He's most likely the only life out here beside us." I always joked when I was scared. And I was scared. What if we ran out of gas, or I had broken an axle in the dry wash we just drove through? Who would know? Who would find us? I glanced at Mom. She must have been thinking along those lines for a long time. "Are you scared, Mom?" If she was, I'd admit to being scared, too.

Mom sat erect, shading her eyes, although she wore a hat. "No need to be scared. We're almost there."

The landscape looked the same to me. "How can you tell?"

"When we drive between those two hills, you'll see the town," she said.

We reached the hills sooner than I expected. The road between them was narrow, and driving it was like driving through a geode sliced in half to display its crystal colors. When we came out on the other side, there were sand dunes casting long gray shadows. Far ahead, a row of trees stood near a farmhouse.

"Trees out here?" I said.

Mom leaned forward. "Those are tamarisk trees, planted for a windbreak. We'll be there soon now. See, there it is, Sand Canyon!"

Although I hadn't expected a city of tall white buildings rising out of the desert, I was unprepared for the small adobe-and-frame buildings huddled at the base of a mountain. The mountain stood like a giant retaining wall behind them. A scattering of cactus clung to the lowlands, as though they could climb no farther. Higher up, spills of rock cut scars through thick dry brush. As we neared, I noticed a sign, Population 5000. Mom smiled. "It's an old sign. This was once a silver-mining town."

The long street made me think I was in a TV Western. I drove slowly. The only movement, other than the Jeep, was a tumbleweed. Silence closed like a vise around us. Dead eyes are watching, I thought, and shivered. I gripped the wheel and glanced at Mom. She had to be wrong. This couldn't be the town. Then I saw faded lettering above a door. Sand Canyon Merchandise. She wasn't wrong. We were in Sand Canyon. But it was a ghost town.

"My, oh, my," Mom said in a soft voice, her eyes misty. "It's just the way Dad said it was in his letters."

I wanted to scream, You knew it was going to be like this and you came anyway? I continued to drive slowly, and silently hoped there was someone here.

We neared a large sun-blistered house midway up the street. I saw the sign I'd been searching for and felt a surge of pride. Dr. Joe Morgan. The sign had a look of dignity and promise. This was the house where the grandfather I'd never seen had lived. A lump came to my parched throat. I swallowed, but it didn't go away. I wished with all my heart that my grandfather were waiting to greet us on the unpainted porch.

A woman appeared at the window of an adobe we were passing. A child came to stand in a doorway across the street. A dog, ribs showing, sauntered toward our slow-moving Jeep. I took a deep breath and let it go as people came from buildings that moments earlier I'd thought were vacant. They stood watching us. They seemed to be waiting to see where we would stop—all but one. He leaped a picket fence and ran toward us. I pulled up in front of the house that would be home, hospital and office to Mom for the summer, and a prison for me.

A deeply tanned boy opened the car door for Mom and removed his hat. His smile was brilliant, and as much as I wanted to believe he was the doctor my grandfather had sent through medical school, I knew he wasn't. For all his desert ruggedness, he was no more than two or three years older than I.

"You came. I didn't think you would," he said.

"Yes, I came," Mom said, getting out. "You must be Allen Hasting."

He nodded. "I guess Dr. Joe told you about me." He looked pleased.

"Yes, and he said you were a big help to him."

"I'm glad." Allen started around to open my door, but I got out before he reached it. I saw that he was taller than I was and that he had dark penetrating eyes, which were studying me with frank admiration. The last I must have been mistaken about. I was red with every freckle I'd ever discovered blooming, and my brown hair stuck to my cheeks and forehead. I reached up and tugged my wet blouse away from my body.

"My daughter, April," Mom said.

"April." Allen rolled my name the way the tumbleweed rolls with a certain casual beauty. "April is when the wildflowers are in bloom." His dark eyes stirred a feeling in me that made me look away. For the first time I was glad I was sunburned.

I reached for the largest suitcase. "Too bad we missed seeing them."

Allen was quicker and lifted it out. "You'll see them next year."

The people were closer now. I didn't bother to tell Allen there would be no next year here for me or my mother. I looked at her. For all the hard drive across the desert, she now managed to appear fresh and rested. She was shaking offered hands, touching kids' heads and asking questions. Seeing her so at home in surroundings I disliked and earlier had feared, made me uneasy. But I took a suitcase and followed Allen, who was already on the porch. He took a key from his pocket and unlocked the front door.

I must have looked surprised, because he said, "Dr. Joe gave me the key." He pushed the door open, and the bell over it jingled. "I'll give it to your mother."

"Please keep it." Mom had come up the steps behind us. The townspeople remained in the yard. Mom carried her purse in one hand and one of the three boxes of medical supplies she had brought in the other.

"Thank you, Dr. Edmund, but I'd rather not." Allen dropped the key in the side pocket of her purse and stepped aside.

I also waited for her to enter first. I wasn't sure why. It just seemed the right thing to do.

Mom hesitated, then seemed to brace herself for what was to come by tucking her shoulders back. She walked inside. I quickly followed. Although I knew she'd never been in this house before, she was certain to see things that would remind her of my grandfather, the way certain things reminded me of her. I hoped my grandfather's worn medical bag wasn't sitting around for her to find when she was alone. At least not until she had some rest and something to eat.

"I'll get the air conditioner going while you bring in the rest of the things," she said, and I knew she'd be okay.

Allen and I finished unloading the Jeep. I carried a tightly sealed box of antibiotics and antihistamine. Mom had carried in the codeine and vials of morphine sulfate quarter grain, which she would lock in a safe place. Allen carried the usual medical supplies. He opened the door to the left of the hallway and led the way into a small office, a large desk, two chairs and a glass-front bookcase its only furniture.

Allen took a ring of keys from his pocket and opened a door at the back of the room. I stared in surprise. "These keys are definitely your mother's," he said.

"I would hope so." I spoke without thought. But it annoyed me that Allen was so at home in my grandfather's house, and I didn't even know where the bathroom was.

When Allen went into the back room, I looked more closely at my grandfather's desk. On it was a folder that could be a patient's file, a picture of me and Mom and the coffee mug I had sent him last Christmas. It was a month after he had sent Mom a letter congratulating her on an article she had written on "Knowing your Medication." The article had appeared in a national magazine. Until then, Grandpa had been someone I sent a Christmas card to. Mom sometimes included a note. I knew that he was in California and planned to stay there, and that we were in Washington and intended to stay where we were. After Grandpa wrote the letter, Mom answered, and they had been writing ever since, that is until she got the letter from Allen. There were pencils in the mug, and beside it a small calendar. May 29 was circled.

Allen called, "April, come on. I'll show you where I'm putting these supplies."

I ripped off the month of May and stuffed it into my pocket. I planned to find out why the day my grandfather died was circled.

The room I entered was larger than the office and lined with shelves. An examination table stood in the middle of the room. A tourniquet and a blood-pressure cuff lay on a long counter pushed against the wall. There was also a two-row wooden rack filled with glass vials, a graduated beaker and a centrifuge. This was a small lab, but a well-equipped one.

Allen smiled. "Don't look so surprised. Dr. Morgan not only kept up with what's going on in medicine, he never forgot the old ways, either. Once, when I was with him, he stopped the Jeep, and we gathered sage leaves for tea for Miss Sara. She thinks it helps her arthritis."

I tried not to show my feelings, but the words slipped out. "I wish I'd known him." I heard how sad they sounded.

Allen took a step toward me. "I guess I can answer most things you want to know about him."

"I'll keep it in mind," I said, and lifted my damp hair from my sweaty neck. I hoped the act would be taken as one of casualness. The annoyance I'd felt with Allen for being at home in my grandfather's house was nothing compared to the jealousy I felt at his considering himself an authority on Grandpa.

I walked from the room before I could say something mean. Mom stood by Grandpa's desk, her fingers moving across it the way a person reads braille, her eyes filled with memories I'd never shared.

I tried to get out without disturbing her, but she smiled at us. "He must have had a difficult time getting this old desk here. My mother gave it to him when he started his practice. He never said so, but he must have loved it very much."

"It's a good strong desk," Allen said.

What a dumb thing to say, I thought. But I couldn't think of anything better. I just stood there wanting to escape my mother's sad face.

Allen fished in his pocket and came up with the ring of keys again. "Doctor Joe got into the habit of leaving these with me. He left them with me that day." I saw his cheeks redden despite his tan. Why, Allen hated all this! He probably hated us for intruding into my grandfather's world. Maybe he wondered why we had never visited him when he was alive and had come prying now that it was too late to help him.

"Allen," Mom said. "I want to talk to you about that day."

"I know," he said. "But it can't be now. You've got company."

I looked out the window. Townspeople were coming back, the children now scrubbed, the women in fresh dresses, their hair neatly combed. Each woman carried a gift, a casserole, a loaf of bread, a covered pan. The men walked beside them. Earlier, most of the men had stared at my mother with open curiosity. I wondered how many, if any, would allow themselves to be examined by her. I knew in time she would win them over. She used to say Grandfather was a born doctor and that his patients loved him. He put his own needs aside to administer to the needs of others. If this made a born doctor, my mother was certainly one.

She went to greet the people with a smile, accepting the gifts, then handing them to me or to Allen, thanking each giver. Mom made each gift special. She raised lids, sniffed aromas. She looked at the brown-crusted bread.

Mom was accepted. Everything was going great until she asked a man, "How did you hurt your arm?"

The room went silent. Then he said, "It ain't nothing, doctor. Me and my oldest boy was hunting jackrabbits, and his gun went off. Nicked my arm. It's about healed now."

"I'd like to take a look at it, just the same."

"Ain't no need." He was embarrassed, I could tell. And there was something more. Maybe he resented a woman doctor, although he hadn't seemed to earlier. I looked for Allen, but he wasn't in the room.

"Just the same, I'll take a look at it tomorrow morning." Mom could sound real firm when she was talking to a patient. Sometimes even when she wasn't.

"Thank you, Dr. Edmund," the woman beside him said. "I'm Mr. Martinez's wife. I'll see that he's here."

Mr. Martinez looked at her, his face guarded. The talk started up again, but something was missing. The couple left soon, and gradually others followed. Then there was only Allen, Mom and me left. I saw how bare and shabby the living-room-made-waiting-room really was.

If my grandfather was as good a doctor as Mom and Allen claimed, he could have practiced anywhere. What had kept him here? It certainly wasn't money. What if whatever it was kept Mom here, also? I was no longer sure of what she would do. And we'd only been here an hour. I glanced at her. She had that look of remembering, like somebody who has just come home. It scared me. "Thanks, Allen," I said. "Mom, let's see the rest of the house." But I didn't care if it was the most beautiful house in the world, I was going to hate it.

Chapter Two

Not only was the front part of the house a waiting room, office, combination lab and examining room, but the dining room and sun porch served as a four-bed hospital. The kitchen, now filled with the townspeople's gifts, was probably used for sterilizing instruments as well as for cooking. Seeing the food made me aware of how hungry I was. "I'm starved," I said, breaking off a chunk of bread and stuffing it into my mouth. Mom continued to look in cupboards. When she opened the door to what appeared to be a broom closet, I asked, "What're you looking for?"

"Nothing. Everything." Another one of her contradictions.

"This casserole is still warm," I said. "The house will wait. I'm not sure my stomach will." I broke off another chunk of bread.

She pushed a drawer shut. "You're right. We've a long time to explore."

"Two months," I said, to remind her of the time limit we'd agreed upon. I cleared a space on the table.

She took two plates from the cupboard. "Mom's old dishes," she said, gazing at one.

I filled my plate with ham, roast beef and beans. After a while Mom started eating, too, but she kept looking around, as though discovering things that pleased her. It made me feel uneasy again.

"Finished?" she asked.

"Finished." I cut a piece of chocolate cake. Chocolate gave me zits. But the only person I'd seen near my own age was Allen, and he wasn't somebody I'd give up chocolate cake for. I thought of Jerry. If I were home just then, I'd have been at a barbecue or out cruising.

"April," Mom said. "Help put this food away."

"Sure." I shoved the last bite of cake into my mouth and picked up the bread and a jar of homemade jam. The pantry smelled of sage and other spices. Its shelves held jars of home-canned fruits and vegetables. For a moment I felt cozy, the way I did mornings when I didn't have to get up right away and could pull the covers around me. Determined not to like it here, I hurried out and closed the pantry door. "Let's check the place out," I said.

Mom put the last of the food in the refrigerator. "Let's," she agreed.

To my surprise, the door leading to the stairwell was locked. Mom tried the key Allen had given her, but it didn't fit. She then pulled out the ring of keys, and dropped the lone key into her pocket. "I'll give this one back to Allen," she said.

"Why are you giving him a key? Why not give it to me?" This Allen was proving to be a real pain.

"You'll get a key. But the lower floor should be open to those who need help. And Allen seems capable."

"I don't see what's so capable about him." I was letting that green-eyed monster out again and showing it as usual.

Mom looked at me questioningly. "April, I've never known you to act like this. You don't even know Allen."

I could tell she expected me to explain. I shrugged. "He thinks he's so smart." I couldn't say Allen and I had gotten off to a bad start because of Grandfather. It might remind her of how she had never visited Grandpa.

She tried different keys on the ring. "Let's give Allen a chance. Okay?" When I didn't answer right away, Mom glanced at me. "Okay?" she said firmly.

"Okay, but my heart won't be in it."

"Good. You're too young for a heart involvement."

"Allen would be the last person . . ."

The lock clicked. "It worked!" Mom said, and pushed open the door.

I stared at the narrow stairwell with a small window at the landing. Sunlight, through the grimy pane, edged dark shadows. The musty odors of a place long-sealed drifted out. "I don't think Grandpa used the upstairs," I said.

"Maybe not. But we're going to use it." Mom led the way.

I stopped at the landing and looked out the window. The desert floor spread to the hills we had driven between, and to the mountains on my right. The question ran across my mind again, what kept my grandfather and these people here?

"Don't you want to see your room?" Mom asked from the top of the stairs.

"For sure," I answered, running up the last flight of steps. "But I already know it'll be gross."

"April, please," she said softly. "You agreed to come. You even wanted to."

"Sure, Mom. It's going to be great," I lied.

The first room looked out on the view I'd seen from the landing window. There was a bed, a chair and a small table in the corner. The room directly across from it had a brass bed, two cane-bottom chairs, a table, a dresser and a bookcase with medical books. Both rooms were draped with cobwebs and layers of dust and fine sand.

"It's been forever since anybody has been up here," I told Mom. The feeling of fear I'd had in the desert returned. Surely my mother must have felt it, but she didn't seem to.

"Let's get right to work," she said, sitting on the bed. The springs squeaked, and dust rose from the patchwork quilt. She looked up and smiled. "Which room would you like?"

"My room at home," I said. "But since I can't have it, I'll take this one. This room faces the street, and I can warn the town when the bad guys ride in." I looked out the window. Nobody was in the street below. "In case there is anybody to warn," I said.

She came to stand beside me. "Before you make a choice, I think we should look in the room at the end of the hall. You might have a better view there."

"Or better bed. Then again, maybe it's the bathroom."

"Let's find out."

I followed her into the hall. When I passed an open door, I said, "It's not the bathroom, not unless there're two up here."

The door was locked. Mom looked surprised, but started trying keys on the ring again.

"Grandpa sure had a thing about locking doors," I said, to ease a mounting tension.

The third key fit. She pushed the door open. I heard her intake of air and saw the way she stiffened. "Let me see," I said, and eased around her. I stopped just inside the door. The room had pale blue walls, a four-poster bed, a rocking chair, a vanity and a bookcase. The furniture was painted white. The blue coverlet and white fluffy pillows looked new. Certainly they had never been used. There was almost no dust. I turned. Mom must have been as surprised as I. Her face was as white as one of the fluffy pillows, and tears were running down her cheeks. "Mom! What's wrong?"

Her lips formed the words. "He moved my room here the way he did his desk. He knew I'd come back one day."

I put my arms around her and felt her sadness flow through me. I hated this house that held answers to questions I wasn't ready to ask.

I stood wanting to console her but not knowing how. She had never talked about growing up. And I wondered now why I'd never asked her.

She pulled free. "April, coming here has been difficult for both of us. Perhaps we should sleep downstairs tonight. Tomorrow we'll move your things in here."

"But Grandpa saved it for you."

She brushed my hair from my damp cheeks and smiled at me. "He saved it for a very young girl with big dreams. He'd be as pleased as I to have you use it."

I looked at the bookcase filled with worn medical books, and wanted to say, I don't want big dreams. I just want to be pretty and have boys like me and not grow any taller.

Mom ran her hand across the back of the rocker. "I treasured the things in this room. You do want to use it?"

"Sure, Mom. It's really neat. Come on. I'll make us a strong cup of tea." I linked my arm with hers. We went back down the dimly lighted hall.

At the bottom of the stairs she turned and locked the door. I was glad that at least a part of this house was going to be ours alone.

"Dr. Edmund," Allen called, as he opened the front door. He held a large kettle.

"Come in, Allen," Mom said, and smoothed her hair. Her face was serene, without a trace of her earlier tears.

I blew my nose and rubbed my eyes. Both were sure to be red.

Mom took the offered kettle. "I'm glad you came back, Allen," she said.

"Miss Sara sent it. She said to tell you she would have brought it herself, but for her arthritis."

"Thank her for us and tell her I'll be by tomorrow morning to see her," Mom told him.

"She'll be pleased." He glanced at me, and his expression changed to one of curiosity. I looked away.

Mom fished the key from her pocket. "I want you to keep this." When he was about to protest, she said, "The doctor needed someone when he wasn't here. And I'll need someone, also."

He put the offered key in his pocket. "I'll take good care of it, Dr. Edmund."

"I know you will. Now, come have tea with us. April was just going to make some. There's even chocolate cake left."

I had to be satisfied with the promise of a key of my own and the fact that this one didn't open the stairwell door or the lab. At least she hadn't trusted Allen with medical supplies. She had taught me to take temperatures and blood pressures, but always rechecked my readings. I would act as a receptionist here. Mom took for granted I'd be a doctor. But I wasn't sure what I wanted to be.

I flipped my hair away from my face and went into the kitchen. At least there were some things Allen didn't know.

I put the teakettle on the hot plate. Mom and Allen sat at the kitchen table. She cut him a piece of cake. "How long have you lived here?" she asked.

"Since I was a kid. I went to grammar school at the end of town. And to high school in Bishop. It's only an hour and a half away. Now I go to State College and come home at semester break. I'm here for the summer."

"Your parents must be pleased to have you home," Mom said.

He laughed. "My parents live in New York. I live with Miss Sara. She's my mother's sister."

The teakettle gave a shrill whistle. I took it from the hot plate, rinsed out the teapot with some of the hot water and used the rest to fill it, then dropped in two tea bags and set it on the table. While I munched a cookie, I wondered what Allen saw in this town that kept him coming back.

He turned to me. "We're a family here with a single purpose."

I crammed the cookie in my mouth. It was bad enough to have him know all about Grandpa, but was he going to read my mind as well? I thought about Jerry and his band, just in case Allen could read minds.

I wished he would tell us what the purpose was that held him and these people here. But he didn't, and Mom didn't ask.

We sat a moment in an awkward silence. Then Allen said, "Mrs. Carpenter makes a really good cake."

Mom put her cup down. "Yes, she does."

I tensed. I knew by her tone of voice that she was going to ask about Grandpa, and I didn't want her to. No matter how calm she looked sitting here smiling at us, she was upset. And I didn't want her more upset. I tried to think of a way to stop her.

"Allen, about that day?"

It was too late, she had asked. For the first time I noticed how hot and old the kitchen was. "Mom!"

"It's all right, April." Her voice was even, controlled.

Don't tell her, I thought, hoping Allen would read my mind. It's too soon. She's too tired to handle it. I concentrated hard.

Allen washed down the last of his cake with hot tea and pushed back his chair. "He always told me where he was going. Only that day, he didn't. I found out later that he hadn't told anyone."

"What about his appointment book?" Mom sounded the same. But I knew how hard this was for her.

"He didn't have one. He relied on his memory. He had a good one."

He hadn't relied on his memory for one appointment. I slid my hand in my pocket to make sure the calendar page was still there. It was.

"They found his Jeep partly buried in sand."

"And he wasn't with it?" She was watching his face for some clue.

"No. If he'd have stayed with it, he'd have been found. You can spot a vehicle from the air. Any desert man knows you stay with your car." He looked perplexed.

"What would make him leave the Jeep?" I asked, forgetting I'd promised myself not to ask him anything since he was such an authority on everything.

"Maybe he was hurrying to a critically ill patient, and the Jeep got stuck in the sand," Mom said.

I turned to Allen again. "Who's been really sick around here?"

"That's just it. Nobody has!"

"The letter said he wasn't found until two days later. There must be more." She was slightly paler, but that was all.

"It's a big desert. He was under some mesquite brush, probably crawled under to get out of the sun."

There was something... something Allen wasn't saying. I felt a shiver of warning like I'd had in the desert. Something was wrong here. I could feel it.

A hot wind blew the back door open. I went to close it. "Maybe now it will cool off."

"Very little," Allen told me. "This is our four o'clock wind. We get it every day."

Thank you, Allen, I thought. Talk about anything but about my grandfather lying dead under desert brush.

"Did he have his medical bag with him?" I'd never heard Mom sound this calm, not even when she told a person of a loved one's death.

"Yes, he had it beside him, Dr. Edmund."

"He was out on a call," I said, wanting to stop Mom from punishing herself.

"April's right," Allen said. "And his Jeep got stuck in the sand."

For a moment I thought Allen would say more, but he didn't.

Mom gripped the table. "Then if he were going to see a patient, maybe that person can tell us something."

"If we knew who the patient was. There're a few houses out there. But most are vacant during the summer months. It gets too hot."

"He spoke of a ranch in one of his letters," she said.

"The Medford ranch. I asked there, but no one had been sick in weeks." Allen leaned forward. "What did Dr. Joe say about the ranch?"

I thought, What business is it of yours? But Mom was frowning, trying to remember, and I knew she would tell him if she could. "He said it was an up and coming ranch. And that in time it would upgrade the townspeople's standard of living."

Allen stood. "That letter must have been written some time back." He pushed his chair in. "Is there anything I can help you with before I leave?" I could tell the mention of the Medford ranch had disturbed him.

"Thank you, no. We're going to sleep on the sun porch tonight and start fresh tomorrow."

"Then I'll come by tomorrow," Allen said, and started for the door.

Mom never moved, but her question stopped him. "Allen, do you think there's a chance it wasn't an accident?"

I caught my breath. She hadn't hinted until now that she thought it could be anything but one.

I saw Allen tense before he turned, but his face showed none of this. "It was an accident, Dr. Edmund."

"I just can't make myself believe my father would be so careless as to leave his Jeep. He knew the desert."

For a moment I thought Allen would tell her what he knew about Grandpa's death. But he only said, "Nobody ever completely knows the desert," and left.

I wanted to shout after him, Maybe nobody knows the desert. But I will know where Grandpa was going that day before I leave here. I put the rest of the cake in the pantry and washed the dishes.

When I finished, I found Mom making up two beds on the sun porch, and helped her. Neither of us spoke of Allen or of Grandpa.

Chapter Three

I finished making my bed and started to draw the short muslin drapes across the sun-porch windows.

"Let's leave them open," Mom said.

"Why not?" I noticed that slow-moving shadows had softened the desert's harshness, yet heightened a foreboding loneliness.

Mom came to stand beside me. "Beautiful, isn't it?"

I looked at the land that challenged and frightened me. "You have to be kidding."

"A lot of artists would agree with me." She put an arm around me and gave me one of her rare hugs. "Give it a chance, April. Now let's go outside. Maybe with the sun gone, it'll be cooler."

"I hope you're right." I brushed the back of my

hand across my moist brow and walked toward the front.

"Let's sit out back."

I glanced at her. "I'm glad to see you're not yet ready to start your free medical practice."

She gave me a playful swat on the backside. "April!"

I laughed and opened the screen door to a patch of porch with three open steps leading down to a bare sandy ground. A weathered rocking chair and a small bench were pushed under the eaves where the house extended beyond the porch. The extension hid the chair and bench from view on the right. To the left a high rock fence went well beyond the house next door. A circle of white rocks enclosed a cactus garden. A lone tamarisk tree swayed in the hot wind. Ahead was open desert and distant hills that were turning from purple and gray to black.

Mom looked at the cactus encircled by rocks. "Dad always loved flowers."

Hearing the sadness in her voice I said, "The desert is covered with wildflowers in the spring, if we are to believe Allen."

Mom sat in the rocker. I plopped down on the bench. A ribbon of hot wind whipped across my face, lifting my hair.

Neither of us talked. I was busy sorting my thoughts and feelings. They were one big lump of resentment. And why not? I'd been cheated out of an entire summer. And my sixteenth summer at that.

I leaned against the house that still held the heat. "Mom," I said, "I used to wonder what it would be like to visit Grandpa. But I never expected to really come here." I had been so careful to protect Mom from thinking about Grandpa, and now I had brought up the subject.

But she didn't seem to care that I had. "So did I." When she leaned back, the chair creaked. "I kept telling myself I'd take the time to come. Only I never did. Isn't the desert lovely?" They were practically the same words she'd used inside. Mom was trying hard to make me like it here.

A lizard scurried across the sand. "Will you settle for different?" I asked, and we both laughed.

Somewhere, someone was playing a guitar, the music mingling with talk and laughter. I wondered how often my grandfather had sat where Mom was sitting and Allen had sat on this bench while they talked about their day. I tried to push Allen from my thoughts, but he stayed wedged between me and my grandfather. This could be why I didn't really like Allen. He had all the memories of Grandpa that I wanted. But I also knew that there were little things that made me not trust Allen completely.

I looked at Mom, wanting to ask her questions about Grandpa, but I didn't. We stayed where we were until the town grew quiet again and stars created a rhinestone sky, then we went inside.

I helped her lock up and crawled into bed. The occasional yelp of a coyote broke the night stillness. Finally, I turned on my side, pushed my pillow into my stomach and curled around it. Tomorrow I'd start marking off the days until September.

I awakened with a start, thinking Mom had turned on all the lights. Sun blazed through the sun-porch windows. We had forgotten to draw the drapes. The other bed was stripped, and the covers neatly folded. I got up and went to brush my teeth and to wash. When I came into the kitchen, Mom in blue jeans, her hair tucked under a bandanna, was making breakfast.

"It's going to get hot soon," she said. "We'd better start cleaning the upstairs right away."

"I thought you were going to visit Miss Sara first?" I reminded her, hoping to prolong going back upstairs.

"It's still too early for that. But I've unlocked the front door. So perhaps you'd better dress."

The bell over the door jingled. I ran to the sun porch, put on white shorts and a blue top, slid into my sandals and returned to the kitchen.

Allen was sitting at the table drinking coffee and talking to Mom. He looked up as I entered. "Hi. Sorry I caused you to leave your cereal."

I glanced at the soggy cornflakes and cold toast. Today wasn't starting any better than yesterday between Allen and me. "I thought you were a patient."

"I'm here to help," he said.

Mom picked up her cereal bowl. "Hurry and eat, April. Allen says patients start coming in around nine."

"Mom, it's seven-thirty, practically the middle of the night for summer vacation."

"You can sleep when we get settled." She washed the bowl and put it away.

I wanted to tell her I'd never be settled here. And to tell Allen that we didn't need his help, but we did. I'd have to stay out of his way. If we worked together, he'd be sure to make me mad.

Allen finished his coffee and stood. "Before we start, there's something I'd like to show you, April."

"Later. Let's get the work done first," I said, and hurried to the sun porch.

Allen followed me without protest. Getting no opposition, I found myself wishing I had gone with him and wondering what it was that he wanted me to see. It was too late to change my mind. He picked up Mom's suitcase and started toward the stairwell door. I followed him with my own. Mom had already unlocked the door. She carried a bucket, detergent, two brooms and some rags. She glanced at me. "April, you shouldn't be wearing those white shorts. They'll just get dirty. Oh, never mind. I saw an old shirt of Dad's upstairs. You can put it on over them."

She led the way. Allen was behind me. Annoying as he was, I was glad that it was he, not I, carrying Mom's heavy suitcase.

Allen stopped at the landing. "I've never been up here." He sounded curious.

I turned. "I thought you knew everything about my grandfather's house," I said, feeling the tang of my first victory.

"Not really. If I couldn't find Dr. Joe downstairs, he could usually be found outside.

I went up the last steps hoping we had left the door at the end of the hall closed. It was open. "I'll put my case in my room," I said, and was glad when Allen didn't follow me. If there were things about this house that he didn't know, I wanted to be the one who discovered them.

I put my suitcase in the room and hurried out, closing the door behind me. Whatever Mom said, that room was intended only for her. Still, I couldn't help wondering what secrets it held.

Gray swirling dust came from the front bedroom where Allen was working. Mom's voice was coming from the one that faced the desert. She was singing a song I'd never heard.

"I don't think it will be a gold record," I said.

She smiled and threw a nearby shirt to me, saying, "This should protect those shorts."

"You told me he was tall, but this tall?" I said, learning still another thing about him. Only my fingertips showed beneath the cuffs, and the shirt more than hid my shorts.

Mom's eyes clouded. "He was a big man. Not many but me would argue with him."

Cobwebs clung to my hands as I removed rotting curtains from the grimy windows. "How come you never told me much about Grandpa?" I asked, wondering if an argument had parted them.

"There wasn't that much to tell. We were both strong willed. Neither of us would give an inch. He was a leader. Maybe we both were. Patients followed Dad's advice without question. But not me. I always stood up to him and did the opposite. Perhaps if I talked to him the way you talk to me, things would've been different."

I had taken her earlier joy away, and I wanted to give it back. "But you did what he must have wanted when you became a doctor. What was that song you were singing?"

"Oh, just a song your grandfather taught me long ago." She took long firm sweeps with her broom.

"Sing it again, please."

She began to sing, and some of her earlier joy seemed to return. Mom liked it here. Suppose she decided to stay the way Grandpa had stayed? To remind her of her duty to her patients at home, I asked, "Mom, is Dr. Ross a good doctor?"

"The best. I just might go back and find I've lost all my patients to him." She didn't sound worried.

But I had to be satisfied with knowing that, for now, she intended to leave here in September. All I had to do was find a way to last until then.

I mopped the floor when the dust settled, and Mom washed the windows. Once, I caught a glimpse of Allen across the hall. He was shirtless, and his back was baked brown from the desert sun. Perspiration made his muscles glisten. A funny little catch came to my throat, and I quickly looked away.

It was almost nine and the heat had turned the upstairs into a furnace, when Mom looked at her watch. "Let's call it quits," she said, pulling off her bandanna and using it to pat her forehead.

I fluffed her bed pillow and put it into place. The room didn't look too bad. It certainly wasn't home, but it was okay for a few weeks. And anyway, I didn't want it too nice. Mom might get ideas about staying. As it was, she seemed elated with the results.

I went across the hall to tell Allen it was time to quit.

He was sitting on the floor, studying one of the worn medical books. A flame of jealousy flared up in me. Allen didn't have to be pushed into medicine. He loved it the way my grandfather had. The way my mother did. And because he did, he had moved into my grandfather's life. And now he would move into my mother's, too. I won't let you, I thought. I smiled, to mask my feelings, and waited for him to discover me. When he didn't, I asked, "What are you reading?"

"Something dull," he said, snapping the book shut and standing.

This was a better room than the other, the furniture, bed, everything about it. I wondered why Mom had chosen the one she did. Whatever her reason, I was glad. She wouldn't be as comfortable there.

Allen reached for his shirt. "I'm finished in here."

"Mom wants us to quit for the day," I said, wishing he would put his shirt on and wondering why I wanted him to.

Mom offered to pay Allen, but he refused. She glanced at her watch. "April, I'm going to take a quick shower. I want to visit Miss Sara before seeing my first patient."

Allen followed her downstairs, and I went to the room to change. It seemed no more my own than it had earlier. I found myself wishing we had continued to sleep on the sun porch and left the upstairs closed the way Grandpa had done. This was strange, because I would have thought I'd be glad to sleep in a room filled with my mother's childhood things. Maybe it was because I kept thinking of Grandpa and of Mom and of how they could no longer mend their differences. I put on a blue sundress, brushed my hair and went downstairs.

I expected Allen to be gone, but he wasn't. "I waited to show you . . ." He stopped.

Mom came out of the downstairs bathroom in a simple white dress and sandals. Her short hair was neatly brushed, and she wore lipstick. I saw the way

Allen was looking at her and wanted to tell him her age.

Mom picked up Miss Sara's scrubbed kettle that Allen had brought our soup in and started out. "Mr. Martinez will be my first appointment," she told me, and left.

"Now that she's gone," Allen said, "come with me. Remember, there was something I wanted to show you."

I hung back. "I'd better stay here."

Allen looked annoyed. "We're only going to the shed outside. You can hear the phone and bell from there."

"Okay." My curiosity got the better of me. I wanted to know what it was Allen was so determined to show me.

We went out the front door to the shed attached to the house. He opened the doors, and we stepped inside. At first I couldn't see clearly, or maybe I didn't allow it to register. But suddenly it did. I caught my breath and stared. "My grandfather's Jeep?" I asked, knowing that it was.

He nodded. "I wanted to see your reaction. It hit you hard, didn't it?"

It was my turn to nod. Allen couldn't know how hard it hit me. If I'd been struck with the two-by-four leaning against the wall, it couldn't have hurt as much as this.

"What I want to know," Allen was saying, "is, would it be better if I showed your mother this, told her about it, or just let her find it for herself after she'd been here awhile. Which do you think would be easier on her?" He sounded concerned.

I couldn't take my eyes from the sand-pitted Jeep that made my grandfather's death real. Allen was waiting. I had to say something. "Tell her it's out here. Let her decide when she wants to see it. Maybe she'll want to come out here alone. She's a very private person."

"She strikes me as outgoing," he said. "You're the loner."

I could have argued with Allen on that, but I only said, "She's good at hiding the way she feels. Thanks for showing me the Jeep first. I have to get back to the house. Mr. Martinez is probably already waiting." I walked out.

Allen closed the shed doors. "Mr. Martinez won't show," he said.

"Then my mother will go to see him." I turned away. Closed doors couldn't shut the Jeep from my mind. The Jeep was Grandpa's last connection to safety, to life. What had made him leave it?

Chapter Four

I went inside, still thinking of Grandpa. A woman holding a baby sat in one of the chairs against the wall. She stood as I entered. "Have you been waiting long?" I asked. "I didn't hear the bell."

"Not long." She moved toward me, her eyes filled with worry. "My baby's sick."

When I said, "The doctor will be in soon," she sat down. I saw Mom hurrying down the street. She met Allen, and he stopped her. She glanced toward the shed, and I knew he was telling her about Grandpa's Jeep. I wished I hadn't suggested it.

"My baby's very sick," the woman said.

"The doctor's coming now. What's the baby's name? I'll get her file." Mom was still with Allen.

"It's Katy... Katy Garcia," the woman said.

An old man came in, gripping a wide-brimmed hat. He nodded to the woman and sat on the couch at the end of the room. I asked him his name and went to pull the two files.

Mom came into the office. She took Katy's folder and studied the few loose pages. I watched her expression. She didn't seem upset. Maybe Allen hadn't told her about the Jeep after all.

Mom looked up and smiled. "Dad's writing is as bad as..."

"As yours." I also smiled and went to have the woman and baby come in.

There was nothing more for me to do until I ushered the man in.

We had only one other patient, a Larry Medford. At first, I didn't remember where I'd heard the name. He was the man with the ranch. He had stepped on a rusty nail in an empty house and had come in for a tetanus shot. He was a big man, about Mom's age, with wide shoulders, brown sun-streaked hair and the bluest eyes I'd ever seen. I checked the file cabinet. While I did, he asked me questions about myself and told me it was a shame for me to waste my summer here. He invited me to the Medford ranch to go riding. Grandpa had no file on him. He said he'd been in before, but guessed my grandfather hadn't made up a file. I liked Mr. Medford. Mom seemed to like him, too.

It was past noon, and Allen was right. Mr. Martinez wasn't going to show. Mom asked me to get his address from his file.

"I guess Grandpa knew where everybody lives," I told her. "No file has an address on it."

"I'd better stay here in case another patient comes in," she said. "You run up the street and ask Miss Sara or Allen where the Martinezes live."

I didn't want to ask Allen anything, but I went. The dusty street was empty. Tumbleweeds pressed against fences. Sagebrush sat between buildings. The air was so thin, I took deep breaths to get enough of it. Although I no longer thought of Sand Canyon as a ghost town, a feeling that the dead were all around made me hurry. Maybe I didn't understand why the people stayed, but I soon knew why they stayed inside. In the short time it took to reach Miss Sara's house, my dress stuck to me and perspiration slid down my face. I mopped my cheeks with the back of my hand and knocked.

Allen opened the screen door. "Come in."

I entered a small room that was cluttered the way a room is where needed objects must be kept in one area—in this instance, around a large overstuffed chair. The size of the chair made the woman sitting in it appear small and frail. Her short gray hair and wise gray eyes matched the smock that she wore. When she smiled, her stern face became warm and friendly. "You're April. Allen has told me about you." She reached for a pitcher on a nearby table. "Come, have iced tea."

"Thank you." I wondered what Allen had said about me and didn't dare look at him. She filled one of the four glasses on the tray and held it out. "It's nice to have two visitors in one day."

"This isn't exactly a visit," I told her, feeling guilty that I wouldn't be staying long. "Dr. Edmund thought you would know Mr. Martinez's address."

A look of fright crossed her face. "Has something happened to Mr. Martinez?"

Her reaction so surprised me that I answered, "I don't know. He didn't keep his appointment to have a gunshot wound treated. My mother wants to go to his house and take a look at his arm." I wondered why she had jumped to the conclusion that something must have happened to him.

She stared through the window at the empty street. "The doctor might as well stay in out of the heat. He won't let her see that arm. He's afraid."

"He's afraid of all doctors," Allen said. "He lives in that adobe house outside of town."

"I'll tell her." Allen hadn't wanted his aunt to tell me about Mr. Martinez's arm or why he was afraid. Some secret held these people in this town, and Allen had a part in it.

Miss Sara continued to stare out the window. "It's just a dry lake bed. Why won't he let go? Why don't we all let go? It would stop, then."

Before I could ask her what would stop, Allen moved to put his arm around her. "Aunt Sara, you're tired. You should rest." His dark eyes flashed me a cold dismissal. "Was his address all you wanted?"

"Yeah." I touched her hands, clasped in her lap, and smiled down at her. "I'll visit you soon," I said, thinking, When your nephew's not around.

Allen walked with me to the door. I felt it was more to hurry me than a courtesy. "Tell the doctor Mr. Martinez isn't home. And that I'll go there with her tomorrow."

"I'll tell her," I said.

I walked toward Grandpa's, thinking of how earlier Allen had said they were a family here with a single purpose. Now Miss Sara had said, "Why won't he let go? Why don't we all let go?" Let go of what? Surely they weren't holding on to a few crumbling buildings in the heat, and sandy soil that grew only sagebrush and cactus? Yet that's what it looked like to me.

I had just gotten inside when Allen, in helmet and open shirt, passed by on a dirt bike. I watched him ride into the hot desert. I was almost certain that he was riding to warn Mr. Martinez that Mom was coming to visit him. But why bother, unless Mr. Martinez's gunshot wound wasn't an accident! For a moment it was as though I couldn't breathe. I hurried to find Mom.

She was in the lab, moving small supplies from one shelf to another. I could tell by the sadness in her face that she knew about the Jeep, and I guessed she had seen it while I was at Miss Sara's. Maybe she had sent me there because she had wanted to go to the shed alone. The pain I felt for her swelled in my throat. I swallowed hard. "Allen will show you where the Martinezes live tomorrow," I said. This was no time to tell her something weird was going on in this town and that maybe she was right in thinking Grandpa's death wasn't an accident. She was handling enough problems. I decided not to burden her with more until I knew something for sure.

She kept moving boxes of bandages, tongue depressors, aspirins and other small items that were okay where they were to another shelf. "Dad never did put things where they belong."

It really hurt to watch her. "I'm starved," I said, wanting to get away. When I was upset, I ate.

"April—" She looked at me, her eyes dark wells of sorrow.

"You've seen the Jeep," I said softly.

"Yes, and so have you. Allen told me. But I would have known, even if he hadn't." She picked up a box of cotton swabs. "The Jeep is yours, now."

I sucked in my breath. I wanted a car of my own more than I wanted anything, but not this way. "Oh, Mom, I can't take it."

"I have a car, and Grandpa would have wished you to have it. His monument is a town of living people. He wouldn't want a rusting Jeep as one."

"Thanks. I love you," I said, and ducked out before I started to cry.

I sliced the cake and thought of Grandpa's Jeep and how much I wanted it. The more I wanted it, the guiltier I felt and the more I ate. Finally, I went to the broom closet for a broom to sweep up the cake crumbs I'd dropped on the floor. There were the usual cleaning articles in the small room, and in the back, a narrow door. I knew from having sat in the backyard last evening that it could only lead to a basement, but the door was locked. I got the keys from the drawer I'd seen Mom put them in and tried each one.

I was forcing the last key into the keyhole, when I heard a voice behind me. "None of those works."

I felt as though I'd been caught doing something I shouldn't. "Do you always sneak around?" I asked Allen.

"I came into the kitchen for cake. Your mother offered me some."

"You're too late. I've eaten it." Seeing his disappointment was worth getting zits. I started trying the keys again.

"Dr. Joe told me there never was a key for that door," Allen said in a matter-of-fact voice.

I turned. "You mean the door has never been opened?"

He nodded. "I offered once to break the lock, but he said he had enough space and that if it was like the basements around here, it was just a square hole in the ground. And any steps leading down were sure to be rotted away."

"But wasn't he curious?"

"Your grandfather was too busy to be curious."

Allen was telling me that if I had something to do, I wouldn't be snooping around in a broom closet. I dropped the keys in my pocket. "You weren't gone long."

"Gone?" he sounded surprised.

"I saw you ride out of town."

"Oh, that. Since you've eaten the cake, may I take a couple of cookies?"

"Help yourself. You know better than I where everything is." Annoyed that he had no intentions of saying where he'd been, I turned to leave. The broom closet was smaller than I had realized, and in my haste I brushed against him. The feeling was like an electric shock, frightening and instantly gone. I quickly moved away, certain that Allen had felt it, also. But if he had, he didn't show it. "There's water in the refrigerator, and you know where the cookies are," I told him, and left.

Mom was stacking old magazines. She looked up. "Didn't you see Allen in the kitchen?"

"Yes," I said, going out the door before she could question me. I couldn't explain. My feelings and thoughts were too mixed up. I knew I didn't really like Allen, and yet when I had brushed against him I'd felt a sensation I had never felt with any boy before. More disturbing, maybe Allen was a part of something that could have led to my grandfather's death and gotten Mr. Martinez shot. He certainly knew the reason these people were staying on in their rotting houses. And he wasn't telling. Why should I believe him when he said the basement door had no key and had never been opened? Suppose the answer was down there.

The blast of heat was like opening an oven. I hurried to get out of it. If Allen could visit us anytime that he pleased, I could do some visiting on my own. And I knew where. There were questions I wanted to ask when Allen wasn't around.

A kid in khaki shorts, darting from a house, startled me. I stopped. I would never get used to this town with its hollow-eyed buildings that appeared vacant, yet held families. My eyes stung from a glint of light, and I blinked. The late sun's rays were hitting metal somewhere on the mountain.

I shaded my eyes. Somewhere up there was a mine. I could see rusty ore cars and knew there must also be the remains of a narrow-gauge track for a train. Although I carefully scanned the terrain, I could find no trace of a mine. Again my eyes felt the biting sting of light. Perhaps it was only a tin can or a piece of glass, or was somebody up there? I searched for some movement. There was none.

I was so intent on studying the mountain that I wasn't aware of Allen until he said, "What's so interesting?"

"Can't I go anywhere alone?" I said, feeling disappointment that I couldn't question Miss Sara.

He handed me my old cloth hat. "Your mother noticed you left without this," he said.

"My mother, the doctor." I pulled the hat on. "She probably thought I'd get sunstroke."

"You could. Let's get back inside." Allen looked toward the mountain. "What did you see?"

"I'm not sure, but I think there's somebody up there. The sun reflected off a mirror or binoculars or something." The latter was prompted by Allen's curiosity. But it didn't prepare me for his reaction.

He grabbed my hand. The electrical current was lost in the warm strength of his grip. "If anybody's up there, it's a kid," he said, urging me from the street. "Come on, let's get out of the heat."

"Is that where the mine is?"

"Yes."

I still held back. "I think I'll hike up there. I've never seen the inside of a mine."

"And you won't see the inside of that one. It's boarded up. Old-timers say that some of the shafts are flooded."

"Why would anyone hang around a boarded-up mine?" I tried to hold my ground, but he was stronger.

"How should I know? I told you kids like to go up there."

He hurried me across the street to the rear of a house with broken windows, and a door that hung on one hinge.

I tried to pull free. "Where are you taking me?"

"First, I'm getting you out of the sun, and there's something in here for you to see."

I had to go along with him. Yet I had the feeling Allen knew someone was on the mountain. But again he wasn't telling.

He led the way into the empty house. I followed only because of his firm grip on my hand that was hurting now.

The creaking floor sagged under each step, and dust stirred. But it was the dry heat and smell of decay that stopped me. I looked at Allen to question the safety of our being in there. His eyes appeared dark, and there was a slight pallor under his tan. Something had frightened him. It could have only had something to do with the mountain. I jerked free. "What's going on in this town? Who was up on the mountain?" I hoped my voice commanded an answer.

He visibly relaxed. "Nothing's going on. I remembered this old house and thought I'd show you the basement. And if you've seen one mining-town basement you've seen them all."

I followed him as he walked toward a closed door. I thought, Whatever it is, you're in the middle of it, Allen, and that's for sure.

He opened the door and stepped aside. I looked in. "I can't see a thing. It's totally black down there."

"You won't see any more at Dr. Joe's, so why keep trying to open the basement door?"

I glanced at him, surprised. "What makes you think I'll try again?"

"You had that same determined look Dr. Joe used to get."

I smiled in spite of myself. "I can't see a thing without a flashlight."

"We can always go to your place and get one." He started toward the back door.

"I've seen all I want to see." I hurried to keep up. An empty house has always been scary to me.

"Let's go the back way," Allen said.

"Won't people object to our cutting across their yards?"

He laughed. "What yards? Come on."

I went with him, aware that the row of houses hid us from the view of anyone on the mountainside. I was also aware that Allen's reason for following me, and then getting me out of the street, hadn't been to show me a basement.

Chapter Five

Mom had no other patients, and in the evening we sat in the backyard again. There were so many things to tell her. I wanted to discuss seeing someone on the mountain and Allen's reaction. Mostly, I wanted to talk about the basement. Surely she must have tried the door, found it locked and also wondered why. But instead, I spoke of the heat. I was getting too old to lay all my problems on Mom, especially with her feeling guilty and sad about Grandpa. It was surprising to learn she loved him this much and never talked about him. I guess I shouldn't have been surprised. As much as I loved my father, I'd never told anybody the way I felt or how much it hurt that he deserted us, and how often I wished things could have been different. I guess we were alike, Mom and I. By not talking about our feelings we kept them under control. But Mom was sure close to hers that night. It was no time to say I was suspicious of Allen. She liked him a lot.

"It's peaceful here, isn't it?" she said, her head against the rocker's back, eyes straight ahead.

"You could call it that." I watched the desert change from drab greens and tans to shadowy grays and purples.

As it grew dark, music rode the warm wind the way it had the night before. It was a different song, but still haunting and beckoning. I was more rested and wanted to search it out, but that meant leaving Mom alone. She was unusually quiet, and she needed me close. I could feel her depression. Tomorrow night, I told myself.

I was glad when it was time to go to bed. I kissed Mom, said good-night and went to my room, which was really hers. Seeing the room had hurt her the most. Mom realized how much she and Grandpa had missed because of the silence between them.

I still felt a little uneasy being there, and I didn't know why. I wasn't sleepy, so I pulled a book on sewing from the bookcase and opened it. On the flyleaf, in bold strokes, was, "To Jane on her 12th birthday. Dad." I stood holding the book that looked new. The only thing I'd ever known Mom to sew was skin.

I put the book back and pulled out another and still another. All were old medical books. All were autographed to Mom. The succession in which I checked through them made me aware of the ink. Soon it became apparent that these books had been inscribed with the same pen, probably on the same day. Why? Were they his legacy to her?

Before I fell asleep I thought again of the basement. Maybe it held secrets that would help to mend hurts and make Grandpa real for me.

Next morning, I didn't get a chance to try to open the basement door. Mr. Martinez came in before nine. I sent him directly to Mom's office to wait, then hurried out to find her. She was as pleased as I, but quickly hid her emotions.

I stayed in the waiting room, but with the door open I could hear what the two were saying.

"I can't see no reason for you looking at it, doctor. The bullet went straight through the flesh. I was lucky. So was that boy of mine. Teenager or not, I'd have licked him for being so careless."

"You were lucky," Mom said. "I'll clean it out and put a fresh dressing on it." I wished she had asked him more questions. I walked with him outside and tried a question of my own. "I saw your place when we came into town. Are you interested in selling?"

He glared at me. "Why would you ask a question like that?"

He was really mad. I could tell I'd asked the wrong question. "Some of the houses have been sold, and I've heard rumors . . ." I stammered, unable to finish the lie.

"Well, mine ain't for sale. And you can tell whoever put you up to this the same thing." He hurried away.

I stood trembling. I had learned one thing. Someone did want to buy Mr. Martinez's place. Maybe they had wanted to buy Grandpa's, too. It was a cinch now that Mr. Martinez would never tell Mom how he got the gunshot wound. I'd blown it. But someone in this town knew how he got it.

I glanced toward Miss Sara's. Maybe she knew. Allen waved from the yard.

I waved back. No need to go there now, when he was home. Although Allen probably knew the entire story, it would be useless to ask him. I went back inside and looked in the office. "Mom, I'm going to take my Jeep out."

She looked pleased. "Okay. The keys are in the glove compartment. Just don't go far."

"I won't." She was actually glad. Mom has always said that it's best to get back into the business of living as soon as possible after a death. At the hospital, when she lost a patient, she would visit the nursery to see the newly born. She said it put life in its right perspective.

I slipped on shorts, a top and sandals, then pulled on my old cloth hat and went out. Seeing the Jeep brought a jolt, but nothing like the first one. I got in and sat a moment before feeling in the glove compartment for the keys. It's usually hard to get used to a car, but having driven Mom's made this one easy. I backed out and closed the shed doors again. I'd noticed Allen was no longer outside, and hoped that if I closed the doors he wouldn't know the Jeep was gone.

I drove out of town in heat that stung and with dust circling around the Jeep. I had no idea where I was going. But there was a lot of desert. I'd find a place to be alone, and at the same time feel close to Grandpa. I was sure I'd recognize the place when I saw it.

There was no special place. Everything was the same. How could my grandfather have endured this heat and sameness? I wondered, looking at a blue haze that hung low in the sky and mountains that appeared close, yet were miles away. My throat felt dry, making me aware that I hadn't remembered to bring something to drink. "Dumb, dumb," I said.

I had decided to turn back when I saw a dirt bike leaping across the mounds of sand and brush. I speeded up, hoping the rider of the bike wasn't who I thought. No such luck. Already Allen was frantically waving me to a stop. I didn't dare not stop. Suppose something had happened to Mom?

He came alongside, swooped to a stop and got off. "What are you doing out here alone?" he asked, putting his bike in the back of the Jeep.

"Never mind me, what are you doing? Get your bike out of my car!" Then, realizing what I had just said, I added softly, "Mom gave it to me."

"I'm glad she did." He leaped over the door to sit beside me. "Now, let's go back."

"No." I snatched the keys from the ignition.

"April, you're the most exasperating kid I've ever met. You ride out in the desert dressed like this and acting as though you know where you're going. And where's your canteen?"

"I forgot to bring one," I answered. "But I don't expect to stay the day. Just long enough..."

"To see the place where your grandfather was found. As though you could find it." He was angry again.

All my anger left. "Is that so wrong?" Allen was right. I had been looking for a mesquite bush that looked different from the rest.

He shook his head. "No." He took off his shirt and put it on me, saying, "You'll sunburn in that sleeveless shirt."

Because I was impatient to ask questions, I obediently slid my arms into the moist sleeves. For a moment we were close. I was aware of his bare chest and the warmth of his breath. A feeling stirred the way I had seen a small whirlwind stir dust in the road without a trace of wind.

Allen leaned back and stared at me. "How old are you, April?"

"Almost seventeen," I said, omitting six months.

He smiled. "I guessed you were sixteen. I'm almost twenty."

"Why did you ask, if you knew?"

He shrugged. "At first I thought you were older, then you acted younger. I was curious, that's all."

"Well, now you know." I mopped my cheek with the back of my hand. I had seen Allen's canteen, but was determined not to ask for a drink of water.

He reached over the seat and took the canteen from his bike. "Here. Your mouth must feel like that sand dune."

"It does. Thanks." I didn't drink as much water as I wanted, because Allen took it, saying, "Hey! We still have to get back to town."

I had no choice. Allen's bike was in the Jeep and I was wearing his shirt. I had to go back.

"Well, do you want to see the place you were looking for or don't you?" Allen asked.

I turned and stared at him. "Do you know the exact place?" It sounded unreal. How could he tell one bush from another?

"I was the one who found him."

"Why didn't you tell Mom you were the one?" I asked, trying to hold my temper.

"She would have expected me to know more than I've told her." His voice revealed a temper of his own.

I jammed the key into the ignition. "You do know more." I was trembling with anger, but didn't care.

"Maybe I do. Then maybe I don't. Let's leave it at that. Start the motor, and I'll show you the place I found your grandfather so you won't wander out here alone again."

I turned on the ignition, flooding the car with sound. "Show me," I said, and braced myself.

"Turn the Jeep around, or we'll end up at the Medford ranch." He glanced at the surroundings with a worried frown. I had seen him do that before. What was there to be afraid of out here? You could see for miles.

I did as I was asked and drove in silence. Allen pointed to what looked like huge cactus, saying, "Those are Joshua trees. Historians say Mormon pioneers were reminded of the Hebrew leader Joshua, who held up his arms beseeching victory in battle."

I only half listened while he told how the trees are seeded by desert winds and how woodpeckers drill the trunk for nests. "When they abandon the nest, owls, wrens and flycatchers take over," he said.

I waited for him to stop talking. I'd rather be alone, I thought. What if I start to cry and can't stop when I see the place? I could feel Allen's eyes studying my face as I drove, but pretended not to notice.

"The next time you decide to leave Sand Canyon alone, tell somebody where you're going," he said.

"Okay," I told him, thinking it wouldn't be him. How had he known so soon that I was gone?

As we drove, I thought that one mesquite bush looked like another. Maybe Allen was being the desert superguide to lead me away from, rather than to the place. My thoughts were broken by Allen's unexpected question. "You don't like it here, do you?"

"It's okay if you're crazy about giant sandpiles," I said.

He laughed. "Stop here."

I stopped, hoping he would point out a clump of brush, or say this was where the Jeep was found. He did neither. Instead, with a sweep of his hand, he said, "Look out there and tell me what you see."

I shaded my eyes. "I see sagebrush, sand and cactus. Which did you find here, my grandfather or his Jeep?" Just saying the words, my heart speeded up.

"I didn't find his Jeep. Your grandpa was a long way from it. The Jeep was found from the air. I told your mother that. Look again. Tell me what you really see."

Irritated, I said, "I've already told you what I saw." Without the sound of the Jeep's engine, the stillness wrapped around the car, making me aware Allen and I were alone. I wasn't afraid of Allen, but I didn't completely trust him, either. "What did I miss?" I tried sounding nonchalant.

"The beauty."

"Beauty?" I stared at him.

He smiled. "Don't look at me, but at that low cactus." He slid his arm across the back of my seat and leaned closer to point to a small brown bird. "That's a cactus wren. Its nest is in there."

I looked more closely. "There really is a bird." I watched in wonder as the bird swept into the sky.

"That's what I said."

Perspiration ran down my cheeks. "Can we go now?" Allen could think the desert beautiful and interesting if he wanted, but I never would.

He took his arm from the back of my seat. "I'm sorry," he said, sounding embarrassed. "Dr. Joe and I used to study the desert a lot. I just thought you'd like it, too." He looked at me closely. "Maybe we should go back and come early tomorrow morning when it's not so hot."

"No!"

"April, I'm used to this heat, you're not."

"I'm okay. Honest. We're out here now." I sounded near to pleading and saw it took effect.

"Okay, start driving." He looked grim.

It wasn't going to be any easier for him than it was for me.

Allen no longer tried to point out sights of beauty as we bounced along tracks made by other cars. I wished that he would. The heat and knowing that we were going to see where Grandpa died were almost unbearable. I glanced at Allen sitting straight and silent beside me, a closed look on his face, and I realized it would do me no good to see the place. I could have easily said, Allen, I've changed my mind. Let's go back to town. The words wouldn't come. Something forced me to face what was ahead, no matter how badly it made me feel. I stared at the colorless desert ahead, my tension mounting until I was sure I'd snap into brittle pieces, like the dried bones of the dead animal we had passed. When I could stand the tense silence no longer, I asked, "How much farther?"

"We're almost there."

"What makes you so sure you'll know the place?" I would rather argue with Allen than have this strained silence.

"I'll know."

"I wish you would tell all you know about what happened out here," I said.

Allen looked at me. I could see him from the corner of my eye. "I'll tell you when I know something for certain," he said.

"You think it wasn't an accident. You believe the way Mom does. The way I'm starting to believe . . ."

"Stop up there near those Joshua trees. And don't start believing things when you have no proof."

I'd get proof, and without his help. I slowed the Jeep and stopped where he indicated. The silence closed in again.

Allen got out, saying, "We'll walk from here."

I sat, not moving. My heart beat so loudly I was certain Allen could hear it pounding. The thought spread through my mind. Maybe he had not only led me away from where he found Grandpa, but was now leading me away from the Jeep, the way somebody had led Grandpa away.

Chapter Six

I don't know how long I sat clutching the wheel. I do know I was torn between wanting to trust Allen and feeling I couldn't, not completely. Yet if I didn't trust him, I could miss out on seeing where Grandpa was found and maybe find a clue about his death.

Allen touched my hand. "Come on. You've come this far." I relaxed my hold on the wheel. His hand closed over mine. "You've been out here too long already. Your mother will be worried."

I pulled my hand away, annoyed. "Stop treating me like a child. Haven't you noticed, I'm a big girl?"

He smiled. "I've noticed." He took my hand again.

I got out. My face feeling warmer than it already was, I walked through low prickly brush over the rocky ground. In the distance carrion birds circled in the blue-white sky. Allen's firm grip on my hand reminded me of his strength. I took a deep breath of the thin air, but couldn't shake a feeling that something was smothering me.

Allen stopped near a gully cut by flash floods. I stopped beside him. He released my hand and pointed. "The Jeep was found in this ditch about a mile up from here."

I looked in the direction Allen pointed and wondered how he could tell. It all looked the same to me.

I followed him across the gully, aware of the dryness of the brush we tramped through. I compared my parched throat to that dryness. Allen's canteen was slung over his shoulder. I could have asked him for a drink, but remained silent. It must have been less than fifteen minutes that we walked, but it seemed forever.

Allen stopped. "This is it," he said, sounding embarrassed.

Nearby, clumps of mesquite brush cast shadows on the hot ground. Under the tallest bush was a small pile of white rocks. I'm not sure what I'd expected. I only knew nothing could have equaled this small pyramid tombstone in a patch of black shade. My heart raced, and an aching sadness made it hard to breathe or to speak. It hurt so much, I wanted to look away. I couldn't.

"I put the rocks there as a kind of memorial...." Allen's voice trailed off.

I bit my lips to hold back tears. "We shipped him back East because we wanted him to be next to Grandma," I said, knowing that to me this desolate spot would always be Grandpa's grave.

We stood not speaking. I couldn't stay, yet didn't want to leave. I had expected to look for clues and to ask questions. I did neither. Seeing a scattering of small white stones a short distance away, I walked to where they were and searched through them. I chose a round one with care, and polished it on my blouse. Then I sank to my knees and placed it on the pyramid.

Allen lifted me to my feet. "It was dumb to bring you here," he said, his voice rough edged.

I rubbed my eyes on the sleeve of his shirt that I still wore. "So I cried. You'd cry, too, if it were your grandfather."

"I did cry," he said, urging me away from the pyramid of rocks. Too upset to object, I went with him. I kept rubbing tears away, wishing they would stop.

Allen glanced at me from time to time as we walked toward the Jeep. Once, he stopped and had me drink some water. "I'm sorry," he said.

"No, I'm glad you brought me here. And I'm okay, honest." But I wasn't okay. My legs were made of rubber, and a floating sensation filled my head.

When we reached the Jeep, Allen handed me the canteen. "Take sips from this. I'll drive."

I took the canteen and got in. It no longer mattered who drove. "Why did he leave his Jeep?" I asked, when I could trust myself to speak.

Allen sat, neither answering nor starting the engine. I was ready to ask him again, when he said, "I've wondered about that myself. And why he went toward the open desert instead of the road."

"Maybe it's the way Mom said; someone needed help."

"There's no road, no houses." He sounded angry.

"You didn't need a road to follow me," I said.

He started the engine, the sound shattering the silence. "If someone needed help, why didn't the searchers find a bike, horse, house . . . or him?" Allen turned the Jeep around. "And when I found your grandfather, you'd think I would have found whoever he was trying to help, too."

"What happened on May 29?" I asked. Allen stared at me. I could tell I had taken him by surprise. "The road," I reminded.

He looked back at it again. "You already know it was the date he disappeared."

"But why did Grandpa circle it on his calendar?" I watched Allen's face for change. There was none. It was a strong face. Under different circumstances, I knew I would like the way Allen looked.

"May 29 was the grammar school graduation exercise," he said. "Guess Dr. Joe didn't want to forget."

"Oh," I said, feeling cheated. I'd been so sure the date had something to do with Grandpa's death.

We rode in silence, and in that time I remembered Allen had said Grandpa didn't have an appointment book; his memory was so good he hadn't needed one. Why, then, would he have circled the date of an event that most people in town would attend? There had to be something superimportant about May 29. I glanced at Allen. His grim expression made him look much older. And although hot wind burned my cheeks, I shivered and scrunched down in the seat. It was for sure that Allen knew why May 29 was circled.

"I told you your mother would be upset," Allen said, when we entered town.

I sat erect and slipped off Allen's shirt as we drove toward Mom waiting on the porch. "I'll wash this for you," I said.

"No sweat," he said, and smiled at his own pun.

Mom met us in the yard. "April, you promised not to go far." She was looking at me the way she did when she knew there was more to something than I was going to tell her.

I got out and tried to look casual. "I met Allen, and he showed me where Grandpa was found." Realizing I couldn't pull it off, I hurried past her and up the steps.

"She was trying to find the place by herself," Allen told her.

"Oh, dear." I heard her stunned hurt just before the door shut behind me.

The old house was cool, and the soft whirr of the air conditioner was as soothing as a stereo. For the first time, I felt at home.

I dashed cold water on my face with my cupped hands, but the heat stayed deep inside my skin, the way it stays in buildings and in the ground. After a while I went to the kitchen.

Mom and Allen sat at the table, talking. He had a tall glass of iced tea in front of him. He stopped in the middle of a sentence when I entered.

Mom looked at me with a worried frown. "Sit here, April," she said, and stood. "I'll get you some iced tea." Mom never waits on me—Allen had told her how I had cried out there.

"Thanks, but I've had plenty of fluids. Allen had a canteen." I wondered why he was still hanging around. I sat down. Anything else Allen had to say about me

I'd hear. Mom got iced tea, cheese and bread. As I munched, aware I was hungry, I also became aware that I faced the broom closet. It reminded me of the basement. I began to think of ways I could open the door without breaking the lock. I finally settled for breaking it, if necessary. "Mom, have you seen Mr. Martinez today?" I asked. Maybe this would be a good way to get Mom out of the house later.

She looked surprised. "No. He didn't have an appointment."

"Don't you think you should look at his arm again? A gunshot wound can get infected. You've said so yourself."

She gave me a perplexed frown. "His arm is healing nicely." She stood. "I'll leave you two to your own talk." Mom thought I wanted to get rid of her so I could be with Allen.

I also stood. "Not me. I'm wiped out. I'm going to take a nap. See you, Allen," I said, not looking at him, and left.

I unlocked the stairwell door, but the blast of heat was too much. I shut it again and went to the sun porch. I could hear Mom and Allen talking quietly. Allen and his big mouth, I thought, lying on my back, staring at the ceiling. Then I thought of the pyramid of rocks and the way he had lifted me to my feet, and I got all mixed up about Allen again.

That evening when we sat out back, there was no music, and Mom was even quieter than the previous night. So I told her where Grandpa was found and that I was trying to find the mesquite bush, only I hadn't known I was, until Allen stopped me. She squeezed my hand, saying that the desert was dangerous and that I was lucky Allen had come along. "I think he's spying on me," I told her.

She laughed. "April, you do come up with some of the strangest things."

"Mom, let's open the basement door." I leaned toward her in my eagerness. "There's something down there, I just know it."

She brushed my damp hair away from my forehead. "I thought you had outgrown buried treasures. And anyway, Allen says there's no key."

"Allen says a lot of things. Most of them I don't believe."

"April! Why would you say such a thing?"

"Because it's true."

"Allen likes you. You're fortunate to find somebody near your own age here," she said.

I wanted to tell her it wasn't me but her that he liked. But I didn't dare. Now was no time to talk about Allen or the basement.

Kids at school used to say their communication lines with their parents were down. Tonight, mine and Mom's weren't only down, they were buried. I suspected that Allen had put a wedge between us, the way he had between me and Grandpa. I decided it was best to go to bed early. I kissed her good-night, and she patted my cheek, but I could tell she was thinking of something else.

The heat still clung upstairs in spite of the fans I had turned on earlier. I stood at the window a long time, trying to see the desert the way my grandfather had seen it. And now the way Mom did. I couldn't. Heat, eerie silence and ghosts of those who had died there were on my mind.

Finally, stars faded and the moon bathed the desert in a pale white glow. For some reason, tonight it made me think of Allen. Maybe because of today. I suspected, whatever I'd said, I was beginning to trust him. I slipped into my coolest nightgown and lay on the sheet. After a while, when the night air cooled, I turned off the fan and slept.

I awakened from a sound sleep. The moon still washed the room with light, making it possible to see each object clearly. I lay there aware of the night's stillness and the occasional cry of a coyote. A soft creaking sound came from downstairs. Silence. It came again. This time followed by a dull thud of something being dropped. I sat up, wide-awake, now. There it was again. My mouth went dry, and my heart raced the way it did when I jogged.

The clock on the stand beside my bed showed 2:00 a.m. Somebody was downstairs! I took a deep breath and forced myself to relax. Maybe Mom couldn't sleep and had gone down for warm milk. I went into the hall. Moonlight through the windows of the open rooms cast pale strips of light on the hall floor. Using the wall as a guide, I made my way to Mom's room. I opened her door and saw the hump of her outline and heard her even breathing. Fear leaped inside me. I wanted to rush in and awaken her. But she would charge downstairs, because of her responsibility for the Demerol and morphine locked in a steel cabinet there. It was better that she was asleep.

The creaking sound came from below again. Who could be down there? Allen had a key. He didn't need to be creeping around at two in the morning. He could come in anytime, thanks to Mom.

I moved quietly down the stairs, unlocked the door at the bottom and opened it a slit to listen. Nothing. I let out the breath I hadn't known I was holding. What I'd heard was the old house settling. I started to close the door.

Just then Allen came from the kitchen. He passed through full moonlight on his quiet, hurried way to the front door.

I clasped my hand over my mouth to stifle the escaping sound of shock and watched frozen as the door shut and locked behind him. Allen knew there were no medical supplies in the kitchen. Why had he gone there?

The broom closet. The door leading to the basement!

Chapter Seven

Next morning, the first thing I did when I went downstairs was to check the basement door. It was still locked, but on a closer look I noticed scratch marks around the lock. Allen didn't have a key, or he would have used it. I wondered if he had gotten the door open. I tried to think. What could Allen and the person on the mountain be involved in that concerned an entire town? Mr. Martinez must be in on it, too, and wanted out, and that's how he got shot. Allen had certainly gone to his place in a hurry when he found out Mom was planning to go there.

I was just finishing breakfast when Mom called me. I hurried to the waiting room. "Will you take care of the baby while I examine Mrs. Garcia?" she asked.

"Ralph can watch her," Mrs. Garcia said, and plopped a protesting baby on the lap of a little kid.

"I'll hold her, Ralph," I said. "But stay close by so she won't be frightened."

Ralph shrugged and let me take the baby.

"Do you know where the mine is?" I asked him, when Mom and Mrs. Garcia went into the examining room.

Another shrug.

"Sure you do. All the big kids know."

"I'm seven." He looked toward the office door.

"And you know, don't you?"

He nodded.

"Take me there." When he shook his head, his eyes wide, I added, "I'll give you a dollar."

He didn't say anything, but continued to watch the office door. When his mother came out, I said, "Mrs. Garcia, can Ralph show me the mine? I've never seen one."

Mrs. Garcia took the baby. "Ralph doesn't know where the mine is. The children aren't allowed to go up there."

"I'm sorry. Allen said they often play there."

She frowned. "No child is allowed on the mountain. The mine is flooded and dangerous."

"Can I show her, Mama? I won't go close," Ralph pleaded.

"Ralph, you know climbing in this heat is bad for you." Her look at me said I should also know.

"It's okay, Ralph," I said, embarrassed.

Ralph ignored me. "I'll be careful. Can I, Mama? She'll give me a dollar."

"Ralph." She sounded tired.

"We'll go now while there's still shade on the mountain."

Mrs. Garcia sighed, seeming to resign herself to his wish. "Oh, all right. But wear your hat and take a canteen and put on your shoes."

"Thank you, Mrs. Garcia," I said, glad Mom was in the lab and had heard none of this conversation. "It doesn't look far."

"It's about a fifteen-minute climb. But it's all climbing. And you'd better wear boots. There're a lot of snakes up there."

If she had meant to frighten me, she succeeded. But I had to know what was going on here and if it had anything to do with Grandpa's death. I had to check the mine out. The mine and the locked basement were all I had. Mr. Martinez wasn't talking, and I couldn't trust Allen.

Mom was still in the lab when I left. I looked in and told her I'd be gone for a while. She nodded and continued with Mrs. Garcia's blood work.

Ralph and I walked between two houses, his thin bare legs and sandaled feet in contrast to my jeans and boots. He wore a wide-brimmed straw hat and carried a canteen. I carried one also, proving I learned something from my last experience. We started to climb almost at once. Ralph did little talking, but I could feel excitement that matched my own. When the mountain grew steep, I asked, "Are you sure you can climb to the mine?" He really looked small and thin.

"I can climb," he said. As if to prove it, he darted ahead to scramble up the mountain.

His red shirt my only guide, I struggled through thick brush, worrying about snakes. The heat burned into my back. I stopped often to sip from my canteen and to mop my forehead. This was more strenuous than jogging. Ralph seemed to delight in having to wait for me. He'd point to rocks where a snake might sun and to sharp needle cactus to avoid.

Gasping for air, I finally asked, "How much farther is it?"

"Not far," he said, and jumped from the boulder he had been sitting on and again led the way. There was no doubt that Ralph knew where the mine was. At least Allen had told the truth about something.

At last, Ralph stopped on a small plateau. Ahead were the ore cars I had seen from the street, and in the brush were rusty tracks. We were near the mine, and I still hadn't seen it. Ralph warned me away from a chubby cactus with sharp needles, and then pointed. The rotting boards across the entrance to the mine were partially hidden by overgrown brush. "I would never have found it without you, Ralph," I said. "You'd better go back now." I fished in the pocket of my jeans and handed him the promised dollar.

I thought he was going to stay, but then he ran, jumping and sliding down the mountainside. I was alone in burning heat and awesome silence. I tried to see between the boards. It was too dark. Cupping my face with my hands, I pressed close to a wide crack and hoped my eyes would adjust to the darkness.

The sound of scattering rocks made me turn. Larry Medford came around a boulder. Ralph must have seen him coming and that was why he had left so abruptly.

"We meet again, Miss Edmund," Larry Medford said.

I shrugged. "I was curious about the old mine."

He grinned. "The way the children are."

"Not only children," I said, giving him a look that said he certainly wasn't one.

This time he laughed. "We're all children at heart, April. It is April, isn't it?"

"Yes. I've never seen a mine and wanted to see this one."

"I'd take you on a tour, but as you've noticed it's been boarded up for years."

"Do you think it will ever be opened again?"

"Are the townspeople saying that it will?" he asked, showing interest.

I walked to where I could see the street. Surely he must know the people didn't have the money it would take to reopen the mine. "They aren't saying anything, about anything."

"That's Sand Canyon," he said, following me. "What are you looking at down there?"

"You get a terrific view from here," I said. I could see the house Allen had taken me into. I was right, you couldn't see the backs of any of the houses on that side of the street. Allen must have known someone was up here. I looked at Mr. Medford. "Do you come here often?"

"This is my first time in years," he said. "Since we can't tour the mine, there's not much up here."

"That's for sure," I said. I couldn't explore now. "There's Miss Sara on her porch. I'll ask her about the mine."

"Before we go, the invitation to come riding at the ranch still holds."

Much as I like to ride, I didn't know Larry Medford. "I don't think..."

"Can't you ride?"

"Of course," I said, my pulse quickening at the thought.

"How good are you?" He was studying me as if really interested.

"Good enough," I said. "My cousin and I used to ride a lot on my uncle's farm during the summer."

"Bet you two used to have races."

"Sure. Lots of times."

"Perhaps you can ride in a race here." His tone was casual, but I could feel him tense, waiting for my response.

I hesitated, both from the surprise and burst of excitement. "I've never ridden in a real race," I said. "I don't think I'm that good."

"Let me be the judge of that. You won't have much time to prepare, though. The race is run in the dry lake bed, on the Fourth of July."

"It's at the Martinez place?" I was as surprised at the location of the race as hearing there was going to be one in two weeks and Allen hadn't mentioned it.

"Yes. It's always held there. The dry bed is good flat ground." He told of a judges' stand to be erected and of a trophy filled with silver dollars. I stood caught up in the challenge of the race and old memories that were the best of summers. He turned to leave. "How about coming out tomorrow?"

"Okay," I said, high on the thought of riding again.

"I'm easy to find. Just stay on the road. You can't get lost." He walked back around the boulder. I heard the crunching of brush, then all was quiet.

I stood wondering if he were the one who had been here, or had it been a kid. Ralph certainly knew his way here. My guess was that all the kids did.

I tried once more to see between the boards into the mountainside, but it was no use. I turned to leave, and when I did, I saw a partly smoked cigar in the dirt and picked it up. I tried to remember if Mr. Martinez's chart showed that he smoked, or if I'd seen Larry Medford with a cigar. He hadn't smoked here. But the cigar was fresh. It couldn't have been here long.

I stopped at Miss Sara's on the way home. She looked pleased to see me. I told her where I had been, and she said the mine had been boarded up for as long as she could remember. I asked if she thought there was still silver in it. She said yes, she did, and that now everybody in town thought so.

I was ready to ask her why now, but saw Allen riding toward us. I didn't want to talk to him. I was afraid he would tell by my face I'd seen him in the house last night.

I hurried toward home, only waving when he slowed his bike.

"Mom, guess what?" I said, plopping down in the chair across the desk from her.

She looked up from a file she was straightening. "What? Where have you been? You're a sight. And how did you get those scratches?"

"Ralph took me up to see the mine."

She leaned back and smiled. "Just when I think I've a grown daughter, you pull something like this."

"What I want to tell you is I met Mr. Medford. He wants me to ride in the Fourth of July race. He offered to loan me a horse."

"April!" She sat erect.

"I'm a good rider. You've said so yourself. Anyway, I'm going out to his ranch to ride tomorrow."

"That's good. You've been bored here without your usual summer activity. But a horse race!"

I didn't think "bored" was the word anymore: with Allen trying to break into our basement and somebody spying on the town from the mountain and now Miss Sara saying everybody thought there was still silver in the mine.

The next morning was clear and perfectly still. The sun would soon turn the desert into a furnace, but some night coolness still remained. I climbed into the Jeep and drove down the road on which Allen had stopped me. This time I knew where I was going.

Summer heat had withered everything except the mesquite, greasewood and cactus. In some places the fine sand banked against clumps of cholla or prickly pear. When I saw a fence, I drove along it to an open gate with an arch over it. Medford Ranch was lettered on the arch. I eased the Jeep up the circular driveway to a large house that looked as though it had been carefully lifted from a Southern plantation and placed here among boulders and cactus. It stood impressive and glowing white in the bright sunlight. I pulled to a stop behind a red Porsche.

The sight of horses grazing behind the white fence excited me. I was glad I had come.

Larry Medford, in jeans and a Western shirt, hurried down the front steps of the house. He looked lean and handsome. "April, I'm glad you came early," he said, opening the car door. I was aware of his smooth voice and manner, and that he, an older man, liked me.

"Thank you for inviting me, Mr. Medford," I said, feeling like an embarrassed kid.

"Call me Larry," he said. "I'm sorry your mother couldn't make it. She was invited, you know."

"She doesn't like to ride," I told him, remembering my mother hadn't been mentioned when he invited me.

"She doesn't know what she's missing."

I shook my head and smiled, sharing a love of riding with him.

"Some of my faster stallions are in the lot," he said, walking toward a red barn. I walked with him and climbed up to sit beside him on the fence while he pointed out horses by name.

He caught me glancing at the house and asked, "Are you expecting someone?"

My face felt warm, but I only said, "No. I was wondering if your wife plans to ride with us."

He laughed. "I hope not. I'm divorced. I live here with a housekeeper and ranch hands." He sounded as though he liked it that way.

When my eyes kept going back to a black stallion, Larry said, "I think you've made up your mind. Carl," he called. A young man came from the stable. "Saddle Black Diamond for Miss Edmund," Larry said. His voice sounded different than when he talked to me.

Carl looked directly at me. A chill slid down my back at his expression of hate. With a single toss of the coiled rope he carried, he cut the black stallion from the herd and led him into the stable.

"He's the one you want, isn't he?" Larry asked.

"Yes," I said, amazed that he had known.

Carl came out leading Black Diamond and a palomino. Both were saddled.

"Let me give you a leg up," Larry said.

I stepped into his cupped hands and swung into the saddle. Larry's smooth mounting of the palomino made me think of Westerns I'd seen.

We rode into the desert. I loved the feel of a horse beneath me, and for the first time wasn't threatened by the open space. I guess I was beginning to notice that all life on the desert adapted to the conditions here. Nature favored neither plants nor animals. Why should it favor man? Those plants and animals that endured were stamped with a certain strength.

I glanced at Larry. He hadn't accepted the desert's strength, but instead denied it with his Southern house, red barn and white fences.

He smiled at me. "I knew you'd be a good rider."

"I'm okay," I said, pleased. But after we had ridden some distance, with him pointing out the boundaries of his land and the heat getting worse, I asked, "Don't you think we should turn back?"

"There's something I want to show you first."

I didn't answer. His remark made me think of Allen saying almost the same thing. Thinking of Allen, I felt a funny catch in my throat. For a reason I couldn't explain, I wished it were Allen beside me now.

"Aren't you curious?" Larry asked.

"Yeah."

"It's a fort."

"A fort in the desert?"

"That was my question when I first saw it. The man who built it was Alto Higg. He left town long ago and came out here to build himself a fort. He died before he completed it. A real eccentric."

"Death Valley has its Scotty's Castle, and Sand Canyon has its fort," I said.

"That's all Sand Canyon has." Larry sounded angry about something. "I've heard there's somebody back East who wants to buy the town, but nobody here will sell."

"Who would buy Sand Canyon?" I had thought somebody wanted to buy some of the houses, but the whole town?

Larry shrugged. "Another Alto Higg?"

I laughed. Then, hearing the sound of hooves, I turned and saw Carl racing toward us. We pulled to a stop and waited for him. There was lather on his horse when he came alongside Larry. He said Larry had a call from New York that must be answered immediately. I offered to return with them, but Larry said go ahead. The fort was just over the rise. I could wait there, and he would bring us a picnic lunch.

He turned his horse around, and the two men raced back in the direction from which we had come. I wondered if the call was the buyer for Sand Canyon. No. If Larry had anything to do with it, he would have known who the buyer was. I watched them go with a feeling of uneasiness that didn't leave until I saw the fort from the top of the rise.

The adobe fort had never been finished. Most of its surrounding wall had crumbled and slid back to the earth it was made from. A foundation was laid, and three small buildings had been started. One had no roof. One building, however, stood complete and, after all these years, in good condition, even to bars on the windows.

I rode through the opening that once must have had a gate into the courtyard. I dismounted and, finding nothing to hitch Black Diamond to, threw the reins over his head. I poured water from my canteen into my hand and let him nuzzle it, at the same time noticing that my canteen was almost empty. Making certain Black Diamond was in the shade of the wall, I stroked his neck and went inside the building to get out of the sun and heat.

In the first room there was a fireplace, a cot with rawhide strips, a chair and a broken table, lying on its side. In the kitchen was another open fireplace. On the hearth were two clay pots and a battered iron kettle. Everything was covered with desert sand.

Although the owner had been dead many years, I had a strong feeling that I was intruding, and that this place hadn't been built for visitors. But the thick adobe walls made it cool inside, so I continued to wander through the small rooms. I wondered why Alto Higg had built this fort. Curious as I was, I didn't climb the narrow winding stairs to the lookout tower. Finally, I grew restless and decided to go outside and see if Larry was coming.

The door wouldn't open. I pulled with all my strength, surprised. It was so easy to come in. Why was it so hard to get out? I kept trying. My fright of empty houses mounted until it overcame me. I had to get out. I ran from room to room. All the windows had bars. I looked out into the courtyard.

Black Diamond was gone!

Chapter Eight

I looked out all the windows again. Where was Black Diamond? He had given no hint of restlessness when I left him standing in the shade of the courtyard wall. Had something spooked him? No. I would have heard.

I rushed to the door and yanked repeatedly. Perspiration running down my cheeks, I finally leaned against it and took deep breaths. I mustn't panic. Larry would return any minute now. But what was taking him so long? I waited.

I thought of seeing Allen coming from our kitchen at 2:00 a.m., Grandpa's death, somebody watching Sand Canyon from the mountain, Mr. Martinez's gunshot wound. Maybe I was close to the secret of Sand Canyon, and somebody knew! What if that somebody were here now? I listened for the sound of feet crunching rock in the courtyard. All I heard was my heart pounding. I tried the door. It still didn't open. A noise came from the kitchen. My heart stopped. "Who's there?" I called. Idiot, I thought. You just told him where you are.

Silence. I looked around for a weapon. There wasn't one.

I crept away from the door. When I did, a large gray rat darted from the kitchen directly across my path. I screamed and jumped back.

I stood shaking. Three deep breaths didn't help. You're overreacting, I told myself. Black Diamond has wandered out of view from the windows, and there's an explanation for the door. So you're a little scared. So check the place out again. By the time you're finished, Larry will be here.

Brave talk inside my head didn't stop my heart from racing as I moved from room to room pushed by a nameless fear. All the rooms were empty. I looked at my watch for what seemed the hundredth time—three-thirty. No picnic lunch. No Larry. It no longer mattered why he hadn't returned, only that he would.

Finally, I walked through the opening to the enclosed stairs that spiraled to the tower. What if I had to spend the night here? The thought pushed me up the narrow, suffocating stairwell.

Alto Higg must have been a small man, or at least a thin one. I snaked my way through thick cobwebs and choking dust raised by my own feet. Much as the sticky cobwebs repelled, they proved that it had been forever since somebody had been up here. At the same time, they told me the tower was no place to hide.

With the cobwebs broken, it would be the first place somebody would look.

I reached the tower and gulped air that felt as though it had come from a volcano. The small circular room had three windows not large enough for a kid to squeeze through. Each gave a different view of the desert. Yet all looked out on sagebrush, cactus, boulders and erosion caused by wind and water, the two so mixed you couldn't tell which did what.

The mountains appeared deceptively close, as did Sand Canyon. Off to the right, looking exactly the same in every detail as when I left, was Larry Medford's ranch. I saw my Jeep parked behind the Porsche and wished that I were in it now. I wondered if something had happened to Larry. I shivered and looked down. Directly below were the adobe ruins of the courtyard. Everything was covered by a layer of blue-white heat. I shaded my eyes. There was neither a lone horse nor horse and rider. I kept watching for some sign of either until shadows lengthened and wind howled through the rooms, sending a mournful wail up the stairwell.

I'm all alone, I thought, and too scared to even cry. It would soon be dark. Had Larry sneaked back and locked me in? Was Mr. Martinez waiting here? Allen? Why would I be dangerous to somebody? Yet maybe somebody planned to come back after dark. Somebody I knew. In the distance, a coyote trailed a rabbit, waiting for the right moment to move in. At least the rabbit had the open desert. I was trapped, and felt even more trapped here in the tower.

I hurried down the narrow stairs, ignoring the sticky cobwebs and stale air. Once down, I checked the door again. It still didn't open. The empty rooms made me feel even more alone. I needed a plan, a place to hide. There was no place to hide. An alert coldness came over me. Soon it would be dark. I scanned the room. The chair? No. I'd have to be behind him with plenty of room to lift my arms. I must have a small weapon. I moved quickly to the table lying on its side. Standing on one of the three remaining legs, I pushed against the table. The rotting leg snapped. The table and I rocked, but managed to stay in position.

Elated that I had a weapon I tested the table leg by swinging my arm, then lifted my canteen and allowed the last few drops of water to trickle down my throat. Still clutching my weapon, I settled to wait. Almost at once I was on my feet again, alert to the sound of crushing brush. I moved into position. When the door opened, I'd be behind it. I could step out and strike from behind. A stunning blow was all that I'd need to give me time to run into the darkness of the open desert.

I waited, mouth dry, fighting panic. Time passed. It must have been an animal. I leaned weakly against the wall, my weapon hanging at my side, and continued to wait. Finally, a faint sound. It grew louder. Horses coming full gallop. I ran to the nearest window. The two riders were too far away to see clearly. I could tell that one led a black horse. Black Diamond? Not uttering a sound, I watched as they came closer. It was Larry and Allen. Only then I screamed. "Help!" I was still screaming when Larry threw open the door. He was followed by Allen a few moments later.

"April!" Larry, said, sounding surprised.

Although Larry was first through the door, it was Allen who reached me. I clung to him, crying. "Was anybody out there? Did you see anyone?" I asked in a rush.

"No." Larry looked perplexed. "Why are you still here?"

Allen didn't say anything, but continued to hold me. I think I took him so by surprise that for once he was speechless.

"And where's Carl?" Larry asked.

"Carl?" Realizing I was in Allen's arms, I drew away, embarrassed. It was the second time I had cried with his arm around me.

"Are you okay?" Allen asked quietly. He had a strange look on his face, as though having discovered something he hadn't known.

I nodded, but my body was shaking, and I couldn't make it stop. "I haven't seen Carl," I told Larry.

"I sent him to get you. And to tell you I had to leave at once to meet an important client."

"He didn't come tell me. But somebody locked me in and then led Black Diamond away." I heard the high, excited pitch of my voice.

"Wait, slow down." Larry took me by the shoulders and looked into my eyes, his own serious. "You weren't locked in. The door sticks. There should be a warning sign on it. It's as bad as being locked in. No wonder you were so frightened. And Black Diamond wasn't led away. You forgot to drop his reins. They were still draped on the saddle when he came back to the stable."

I pulled away to stare at him. "That's impossible. I dropped those reins over his head." I tried to remember if I'd heard the click of a key in the lock when Larry opened the door. Screaming, I'd heard nothing.

"What you did with the reins doesn't matter. Carl's fired for this," Larry said.

"It was really stupid to ride out here alone." Allen's voice sounded cold and angry.

I didn't know if he meant to the fort or to the ranch. Before I could say anything, he asked, "Why *are* you here?"

"She came to choose a horse for the Fourth of July race," Larry said, and turned to me. "I'm sorry, April, both about Carl and the door."

Allen exploded with anger. "She can't ride in that race!"

"Oh, but I can," I said. With my fright pushed aside by Larry's calm explanation of what had happened, I could think more clearly. And one thing was certain: Allen wasn't making my decisions.

He gave me a you're-acting-like-a-kid look. "Did Larry tell you it's an anything-goes race?"

"April's a good rider. I think she'll win," Larry said.

"Let's get out of here," Allen told me, starting to leave.

"Good idea," I said. On this we agreed.

As I started to follow Allen, Larry reached out and took my hand. "April, wait. I want to talk to you."

Allen glared at him. "I'll be just outside," he said, going out and slamming the door.

For a moment Larry's own anger flared, then his smile returned. "He's angry about what happened. So am I, and I'll do more than slam a door when Carl returns." He took my hand. "April, I would have come for you myself. But there was only time to grab my briefcase and drive to Bishop. As it was, I was late for the meeting."

"It's okay," I said, and it was, now that I knew what had happened.

"It's not okay. Until now, Carl's always been a good ranch hand. A little moody. I guess what set him off was he expected to ride Black Diamond in the race."

"If I'd known that, I wouldn't have ridden him out here."

"Yes, you would. You two are a winning pair."

Before I could object further he added, "You might as well ride Black Diamond. Carl certainly isn't going to. April, when I returned and saw your Jeep, I thought you had decided to wait for me. Then Manuel said that Black Diamond came in alone. Allen rode up just then. I asked him to come with me to look for you. I thought you'd been thrown on the way back and that something had happened to Carl, too. I am sorry you were frightened."

I shrugged, embarrassed for yelling so loud and crying. "I was afraid I'd have to stay here all night. But I'm okay, now."

"Good. Shall we go?" He opened the door and stepped aside.

Surprised, I stood looking at him, my fear back. A slammed door would more likely stick than one only closed.

He grinned, his hands up in a helpless gesture. "This time it didn't stick. Just when I thought it would. I must put a warning on this door."

I forced a smile and walked out. The hot wind stung, but I scarcely noticed.

The three of us mounted and rode toward Larry's ranch. We rode abreast for a time, then Larry rode ahead. It's difficult to hold a conversation on horseback. And for the most part we didn't try. Clouds, sky, mountains and the desert were tinted with a soft pink glow of sunset. Maybe it was seeing such startling beauty in this ugly land, but my fear dulled. I found myself thinking I had overreacted. Carl, in his anger, had wanted to frighten me. I didn't know anything that would put me in danger. I had asked a few questions. Most of them had been to Allen. I glanced at him. His taut jaw and rigid set in the saddle told me Allen was still upset. I wondered why everything seemed to lead back to him.

I pushed further thought aside and, exhausted, listened to the sound of the horses' hooves breaking the silence. The hot eroding wind whipped my hair and blouse, but didn't cool. Yet, I was content with the rhythm of Black Diamond. We moved as one, his rippling muscles sensitive to my slightest command.

Larry dropped back, and Allen rode ahead. I knew the answer even before Larry asked. "You will ride Black Diamond in the race?"

"Yes."

"It means riding some every day." He sounded excited.

I nodded. My own excitement was hard to control. Black Diamond in open desert, running free.

When we reached the ranch an old man took the horses to the barn. Carl was nowhere about. Larry offered us dinner, but I said I had to get home.

"Today won't happen again. I'll see to that," Larry said. "See you tomorrow."

"Okay," I said, and with Allen's dirt bike in the back of the Jeep and a sullen Allen in the seat beside me, I pulled out around the Porsche and drove down the circular driveway.

"You're going through with it," Allen said, when we were out the arch gate.

I kept my eyes on the road, although there was no need. "Yeah."

"You're crazy."

"How come you were at the Medford ranch?" I asked, ignoring his remark.

"What else. Looking for you."

"Why?"

"You keep doing such kid things, that's why. Anyway, I feel responsible for you."

"Don't do me any favors." I remembered there was something I wanted to ask him. "Was Carl at the ranch when you got there?"

"I didn't see him, but Medford was, and so was your horse. Medford said he was afraid you'd been thrown, that he was just leaving to look for you. I borrowed a horse and came along."

I glanced at him. Whereas Larry fought the desert, Allen, like the plants and animal life, accepted it, growing strong under its brutal forces. His hair and eyes blended with its browns, and even his skin and clothes did. If he got out of the Jeep right now and walked away, he would soon be swallowed up by his surroundings. The way he had of showing up wherever I went scared me. And I wondered why I was glad that he had today.

"You really going back there tomorrow?"

"Sure," I said. Something weird was happening here. Larry, Martinez and Allen were a part of it. But I didn't intend to let it spoil the one bright spot in my summer, riding Black Diamond in a race.

"You are crazy!" he said, and slouched down in the seat.

In spite of the heat and exhaustion, I laughed. "Scared I'll win?"

"You'll have the best horse. The one on the best horse doesn't usually win. He's often blocked by a rider who knows his own horse can't win."

I looked at him, shocked. "That's not fair!"

It was his turn to laugh. "I told you this wasn't your ordinary race." He sobered. "Don't ride, April."

"Are you riding?"

"Yeah."

"Now I understand your concern. You want to block me before the race." I felt both flushed and fierce that he'd thought I wouldn't see through his plan.

What he would have said, I don't know. I hit a small boulder. The Jeep flew out of control. It took both of us to steady the steering wheel and keep the Jeep upright. Shaken, I pulled to a stop. Allen was so close I could feel his breath on my cheek. I turned and looked into his soft brown eyes. The air was so still everything seemed suspended in silence. I expected Allen to draw away; instead he moved closer. His lips touched mine lightly. A wonderful and strange feeling stirred inside me, and I leaned toward him. As I did, his lips pressed hard over mine. A tingling rushed through my veins. I forgot all but the wonder of the kiss. Allen drew away first. His face had a gentle softness I'd seen when he looked at Miss Sara. I had wanted Allen to kiss me. I drew back confused. Never in my wildest thought had I imagined kissing Allen.

Without a word I restarted the Jeep, sending a blast of noise through the silence. Allen slouched in his seat. I couldn't tell his reaction to the kiss. He probably made a habit of kissing. He was certainly good at it.

We rode in awkward silence until a long-legged bird hurried across in front of the Jeep. "Oh, look at that," I said, more to ease the tension than in interest.

"Don't be fooled by his looks. That's a roadrunner. He's the only thing on the desert that will fight and sometimes kill a rattlesnake," Allen said.

After this I looked more closely for signs of desert life. But I was unprepared for the downward swoop of a cactus wren upon a milk-white butterfly, and the snip of its scissors bill.

I glanced at Allen, who was so much a part of desert life. Perspiration slid down my spine along with a little chill.

Allen tried again to discourage my going back to the Medford ranch, saying, "There're other ranchers who have horses."

"But you said Black Diamond is the best," I told him.

"I also said the best horse doesn't win."

"This time he will," I said, and heard the determination in my voice.

Neither of us spoke until I pulled to a stop in front of Grandfather's house. Then, as Allen took his bike from the back, he asked, "Sure you won't change your mind?"

"I'm sure," I said. I saw Miss Sara go around the house carrying the white bloom of the yucca. I'd seen many of these on the mountainside.

"There's your aunt," I said, surprised to see her walking.

"She's taking the flower to the cemetery," he said. "She goes there often."

"It must take a lot of effort," I said.

"It does."

He went up the street, and I drove the Jeep inside the shed.

That night I stayed awake longer than usual. I wanted to listen for Allen's return to the kitchen. Instead, I found myself thinking of his kiss.

Chapter Nine

If Allen came to the kitchen that night, it was during a time I slept. In the morning the door showed no further signs of having been tampered with.

At breakfast, I casually told Mom that I was going riding and would be back before nine.

Mom looked up from the file she had been studying while sipping coffee. "April, I'd rather you found something else to do and that you not even consider entering a horse race. It's too dangerous."

"There's nothing to do around here." I leaned forward. "You know how much I like to ride. And I won't enter the race if I'm not good enough." I didn't say I not only wanted to ride, but that I wanted to ask Larry about the buyer for Sand Canyon and what had happened to him.

Mom sighed. "Oh, all right." She looked as though she wanted to say more. Instead, she turned to Mrs. Willard's file again. Grandpa had scribbled a note on it to watch her blood pressure. Mrs. Willard's baby was due soon, and Mom was concerned. I was thankful that was on her mind, because it saved me from the argument I had expected.

I'd told her about Alto Higg and his fort, but not what had happened to me. I reasoned that if she knew, she wouldn't let me go again. When I saw her worried frown as I left, I wondered if Allen had told her about my terror. The thought made me determined to win the race, so *he* couldn't.

As I backed the Jeep out, I felt surprisingly happy. It was still too early to give more than a hint of heat to come. I took deep breaths of sage-scented air and started humming, Black Diamond and the race on my mind.

I reached the ranch sooner than I expected. Yet Black Diamond was saddled and waiting when I drove up. Carl was nowhere about. Maybe Larry really had fired him. Larry came toward me, his smiling face showing how glad he was to see me. He wore a tight, off-white Western shirt and tighter jeans. He looked great. I knew today was going to be much better than yesterday.

To my disappointment, he had me ride around in the lot while he watched. When I complained, he said, "April, the race is won with your hands and the bit in Black Diamond's mouth."

I didn't believe him, but continued to do as he told me until he called, "Enough. Now for some fun riding."

He saddled and mounted the palomino, and we rode out into the desert. We rode for an hour, sometimes in silence, other times with Larry instructing me in the art of horse racing. The fort wasn't mentioned, nor did we ride near it. I was glad. I wasn't sure I could have handled it.

One thing I could handle, and when the right moment came I asked the question I'd been waiting to ask. "Why won't the people of Sand Canyon sell?"

"I don't know." He continued to look at distant mountains. "The buyer, to my knowledge, has since withdrawn his offer." He turned in the saddle and smiled at me. "Want to let Black Diamond loose and see what the two of you can do?"

"Okay." I tensed, excited and nervous. What if Black Diamond proved too much to handle?

"For now it's all in fun. But I'll teach you to use a crop. Lie flat, head close to his mane," Larry said, and gave Black Diamond a slap.

The horse leapt forward.

I did as I'd been told. My saddle was too big, and the fast start came as a surprise, but I managed to hang on.

Black Diamond ran faster than I'd ever ridden. Rough ground didn't bother him; he had raced on ground like this before. I wondered if Larry had been his rider.

Disappointment at not learning what I wanted to know blew away. Finally, I reined in and stroked Black Diamond's long neck.

Larry rode up, looking excited. "I think Sand Canyon will have a new champion."

I smiled at him. "Do you mean me, or Black Diamond?"

"Both," he said. "You're a winning pair."

We rode to the ranch. Larry did most of the talking. Having enjoyed myself so much, I was surprised that I was eager to get home. Another surprise came when my heart did a flip-flop as I passed the spot where Allen had pointed out the desert's beauty.

I was prepared for an argument at home when I came from the shower. But Mom only said, "April, take this antibiotic to Mrs. Garcia. Tell her I want to see her in a couple of days."

"Okay," I said. If Mom wasn't going to bring up the subject of horse racing, I sure wasn't. I hurried out.

On the way home from Mrs. Garcia's, I met Allen. He stopped me, saying, "You went back out there, didn't you?"

I shrugged. "So what business is it of yours?"

"April, forget about the race. It isn't for you."

"Larry says I'm a good rider. He thinks . . ."

"You won't win." Allen looked grim.

"We'll see," I said, and ran up the steps. Allen's remark sounded like a warning.

Inside, I went to the kitchen and piled bologna, cheese, tomato and lettuce on a slice of bread. When I slapped another slice of bread on top and saw the size of the sandwich, I knew just how upset I really was. "If you want to enjoy any of this summer," I told myself, "you'll have to find out two things. Why Mr. Martinez was shot, and why Grandpa died the way he did."

I glanced at the broom closet and thought of the locked basement door inside. I intended to break the lock. I just didn't know when.

"April." Mom looked into the kitchen. "I'm going to the Martinezes'."

"Okay," I said, and looked away from the door.

"I won't be gone long."

"Take your time. I'll come and get you if you're needed here." I could scarcely wait for her to leave.

The moment I heard Mom's Jeep drive away, I locked the front door and hurried to the kitchen again. I found a hammer and screwdriver and started to work on the basement door lock. Finally, the lock broke, and after a little push the door opened with an eerie creaking sound. Stale air and a dank odor rushed out at me. I hesitated, then took one of the two flashlights from a shelf. I shined its light into the dark pit below. The circle of light raced down frail wooden steps to a dirt floor.

The answer to the mystery of Sand Canyon must be here. Why else would Allen come here in the night? He just hadn't thought of the basement until I pointed it out to him.

My heart beat so rapidly, my breath came in quick gasps. I stepped inside and stood a moment on the landing, then moved slowly down the stairs, brushing cobwebs aside as I went.

I avoided the broken step near the bottom and moved slowly and carefully to the dirt floor below. There I stopped, afraid to leave the steps.

The air was so oppressive it was difficult to breathe. The circle of white light probed the darkness. I could see a series of crudely built wood shelves against the wall. An old barrel stood in the middle of the floor. Everything was covered with layers of cobwebs that looked like the discarded skins of ghosts. Shivering, I moved toward the barrel. I was afraid I'd find a coiled snake or a rodent inside, but there were only cobwebs. My flashlight searched the room again, more slowly.

Four jars filled with still more cobwebs were on the shelves. That was all. There was nothing here! Disappointment churned in my stomach leaving me weak and shaky. I'd been sure there was something here. Refusing to accept defeat, I again searched every inch of the room with the light. Nothing. When I turned to leave, the circle of light swept across the shelves, and for the first time I noticed they were built like a tall bookcase with sides and a back. The only place I hadn't looked was behind them.

Laying the flashlight on the floor, I tugged on the bookcase. It groaned and moved slightly. Encouraged, I pulled and tugged with new strength. The shelves moved a few inches away from the wall. My arms ached, as did my back. Perspiration ran down my face, but I continued to work.

A sound overhead made me stop. Not breathing, I listened. Somebody was upstairs. I let out my breath. Mom was back. No, it was too early. Allen? He was the only one it could be. I had locked the door. He must have believed we were both gone. My anger was quickly followed by fear.

The footsteps were in the kitchen now. I clicked off the light and struggled to get behind the shelves. No use. I pulled harder. The case gave a little more, and I squeezed behind it, just before a light swept across the basement.

"April! Are you down there?" Allen called.

I stood not answering.

The stairs creaked one at a time. Allen was coming down. "Who's there?" This time his voice sounded tense, unsure.

I couldn't have moved if I had wanted to. If Allen could be trusted, why had he tried to break into the basement at night when he thought we were asleep? No. I was on my own, and he was getting closer.

Suddenly there was the snap of breaking wood and the thud of a body falling. Allen hadn't seen the broken step. He must not have hurt himself, because I heard the commotion of his getting to his feet and rescuing the flashlight. The light swept the wall and crossed my hiding place.

I eased farther behind the case. When I did, I thought I felt something cold, but before I could be sure, my arm was grabbed, I was pulled from behind the shelves and a blinding light struck my face.

"April!" Allen sounded shocked. Then angry. "What are you doing down here? Why didn't you answer me?"

I jerked free. "Since you were so interested in the basement, I decided to check it out."

"Me, interested? You were the one determined to come down here. Are you satisfied now that there's nothing here?"

"How did you get in?" I asked, to avoid answering, knowing well how he got in.

"I used my key. I was out at the Martinezes' ranch, and your mother sent me for some larger bandages and iodine."

That would be easy enough to check, I thought. "A basement is a strange place to look for bandages and iodine," I said.

"I saw that the broom-closet door was open. It never is. Why didn't you answer me when I called you?" he persisted.

"I'm tired of your spying on me, that's why."

"Spying on you? You're nuts! Come on, let's get out of here. It's creepy." He swung the light around.

I got the feeling he was more interested than he wanted me to know. "And Mom is waiting for those supplies," I said sarcastically.

"You don't believe me."

"You are bright," I said, and with my flashlight led the way up the steps, careful to avoid the now-missing one.

When we were in the kitchen, Allen took my arm and forced me to turn. "April, you're right. There is something going on here. I don't know what it is. Only that it's dangerous for anybody who does know what it's all about. I think Mr. Martinez knows, but he won't talk, not even to me, and we've been friends a long time. I keep going out there hoping he will."

Part of my anger and fear left. "I thought I'd find something down there. But there was nothing." I wished I wasn't beginning to trust Allen. It could prove disastrous.

"I told you there was nothing down there. I would have known if there were. I know everybody in town and knew your grandfather better—" He stopped, his eyes saying he was sorry.

It didn't help; the jealousy was back. He was about to say he knew my grandfather better than I did. "Apparently you didn't know him well enough to know why he went into the desert. Or do you know something you're not telling?"

He touched my hand. "April."

I liked having him touch me. This annoyed me even more. How could I work and be on guard if I started liking Allen? "You mustn't keep Mom waiting."

He looked as though he had just remembered her. "You're right," he said, and left the kitchen.

I followed and watched him take a box of bandages from a lower drawer in the desk and iodine from another. Allen did know this house, all but the basement. Maybe he knew it, also. No, the cobwebs would have been broken.

When he was gone, I washed and changed clothes. There were questions to be asked, and I knew who might have the answers. And now was my chance. Allen wouldn't be there to prompt her. I hurried out of the house, locking the front door. I rushed up the street in spite of the stifling heat.

Yet even in my hurry to Miss Sara's, I tried to see the dusty street and old buildings through a buyer's eyes. It only made the houses look older and more sun blistered. None was worth saving. Not even Miss Sara's or Grandpa's. When I thought of a bulldozer turning Grandpa's house into rubble, I felt a strange and unexpected sadness.

"Come in, April," Miss Sara called, before I knocked. I knew she was in her chair near the window and had watched my approach. "I was just this minute thinking of you," she added, once I was inside.

I stood embarrassed and a little scared to ask about the grammar-school graduation—the day Grandpa died. I knew I hadn't asked her sooner because it was hard to do. I heard myself saying, "I would like to talk to you, Miss Sara."

"And I want to talk to you. Come sit where I can see you without turning my head."

I sat on a low stool close to her. From there I could look out of the window. If I saw Allen returning, I would leave.

"You have such lovely hair, April. I had hair like yours. Elmo Larson, that was the man I almost married, used to say my hair reminded him of the sand dunes, ever-changing with lights and shadows." She made the sand dunes sound beautiful. And for the time I was glad my hair was light brown instead of raven-wing black or flame red, the way I'd always wanted.

I reached out and touched her hands folded in her lap. "I want to talk to you about Grandpa and May 29," I said, my voice low.

"You went to Larry Medford's. Will you tell me about it?" She seemed not to hear my request, but was caught up in her own needs. "Allen tells me you're riding Black Diamond in the race." Her faded gray eyes took on a sparkle I'd not seen there. Color came to her cheeks. "I rode in that race once," she said, in a sharing-a-secret voice. "I almost won, too. But Elmo Larson was also in the race. And, well, I just didn't have the heart to beat him. Elmo proposed that night at the street dance. And I've never regretted pulling back on the reins."

"Never?" I asked, wondering if she had told me the story because Allen was also in the race. But I decided my being in the race had brought back an old memory, that was all. Allen and I didn't even like each other. And she must have known that. He had told her everything else, it would seem. "And you didn't even marry him?" I asked.

She touched my cheek with a feather-soft hand. "No. He died of pneumonia two days before our wedding."

"Oh. I'm sorry."

"So am I. But I do have my memories, and I visit his grave often. Sometimes just to talk to him."

Embarrassed, I stammered, "I—I'm going to win the race." Then quickly added, "But then, I don't have somebody in it who loves me the way you did."

She gave me a wise smile. "Are you sure?"

"I'm sure," I said.

The knowing smile stayed, but she said no more about the race. She leaned back. "You wanted to know about the twenty-ninth and the grammar-school graduation. Your grandfather was to be the speaker. And as you know, he wasn't there. Mr. Pillberry, he's the principal, had to speak in his place. By the time he was through talking, most of us would have been asleep if it weren't for watching the door in hopes Dr. Joe would come." She moistened her lips. "Later, I heard that after they found him, Mr. Martinez had said, 'Now we'll never know what he was going to tell us about the mine.'"

I moved closer, my heart racing. "Now you'd never know *what* about the mine?"

"That there's silver, just as I told you there was. Now, after what happened to your grandfather, most people believe me when I say there's enough silver in the mine for all of us. It's just a matter of scraping our money together to get the shafts drained, or finding ways to make new ones."

"Mr. Medford said there was a buyer."

"Yes. None of us would sell. Sam, the buyers' representative, left town when he couldn't convince the people there was no silver. The buyers wanted our land, the mine and all mineral rights. Nobody but Sam knew who they were. I know if Sam got us to sell, he would have made a lot of money."

"Did Mr. Medford have anything to do with the sale?" I held my breath and waited.

She shook her head. "No. And he doesn't own any part of the mine or town."

I looked out of the window. "If you had sold, it would have brought the mine back to life and helped this town. People here could really use the money."

"It's their homes. Their town, their mine. It was your grandfather's, too. As for me, everything here keeps my memories alive. I would never sell!"

Her look made me ashamed of what I'd said. Her words brought the ache I'd had when I thought of Grandpa's house in a heap of rubble. I thought a moment, then said what I knew I had to. "Maybe somebody didn't want Grandpa to say what he planned to say that night."

She nodded. "That's what some around here believe." I could tell by the way she said it, she was one of those people.

My fear was growing again. Miss Sara was someone who wanted the people to keep their town. She must have said what she did about Mr. Martinez and the others selling for Allen's benefit. Suppose Allen was working with Sam and the would-be buyers, and that he would use any means he could to get the people to sell. I shivered. Although I had wanted Mom to sell when I came here, I found myself siding with Miss Sara and the town.

"Dear, you can't be cold. It's really quite warm in here. But if you wish, you may turn the cooler down."

"No. It's okay. But I have to run." I jumped up and hurried toward the door.

"I'll be back to see you," I said, and rushed out.

I ran down the street in spite of the heat. I couldn't see Allen now. Maybe not ever again, without his knowing what I was thinking about him.

Chapter Ten

In the days that followed my talk with Miss Sara, I tried to avoid Allen. It was impossible. He stopped by the office, or we met on my way home from an early ride at the Medford ranch. Allen was riding early, also. But we never spoke of it or the race. At times, I was sorry that I had entered. Practice was boring when my saddle was on a bale of hay. That was where Larry had me learn to use the crop. Hitting a horse in the right place, according to Larry, was important and required stretching back. I had no intentions of using the whip, but was grateful for yoga lessons I'd taken that helped me learn this new skill quickly. And when I flew across the desert, with Larry holding a stopwatch, I was grateful for those races with my cousin on my uncle's farm.

After the first week I was riding high, my stirrups carrying most of my weight. And when it was windy, I would lay flat against Black Diamond's back for balance and wind resistance.

I loved the early-morning workouts. While running, it was just the two of us. I'd whisper in his ear, "We can do it, Black Diamond." I knew he heard me. I just hoped he believed it.

A week before the race the judges' stand was erected and the entries posted in the window of the local store. It surprised me to see seventeen entries. That many horses makes a race really dangerous. A horse can kick or bump another horse. The next day I asked Larry if he'd seen the entry sheet. Although I liked seeing my name among the others, I secretly hoped Larry would convince me to withdraw.

"Yes," he said. "You'll have to stay out of the pack. And don't be the inside horse when you make the turn around the boulder for home."

"Boulder?" I had seen a large jagged one on the dry lake bed, but hadn't thought it would be used as the turning back point for the race.

"You will have no problems if you stay away from the inside." Larry dismissed the subject.

"Sure." I thought about withdrawing. But Larry had spent a lot of time training me. And women in town acted as though I had entered for them. It was really Allen and the men who convinced me to stay. Allen's quiet manner and the amused looks and kidding from the others made me determined to stay in.

Miss Sara wore a smile, and there was a twinkle in her eyes when she saw me. I think she was reliving, through me, the day she and Elmo Larson raced.

The race pushed everything aside but my grandfather's unusual death and Mr. Martinez's gunshot wound. They were always there. I wished I could talk to Allen about the town, my grandfather and the race. But I also remembered how he had come into the basement and my talk with Miss Sara. I couldn't trust Allen. He could be the reason for the anxiety I felt about the race.

The night before the race, Mom and I sat out back as usual. The town was quiet in its final preparation for the next day. I wondered if other riders felt tense, the way I did.

Suddenly, the soft sounds of a guitar floated through the air, the clear and haunting music reminding me of colorful balloons set free. I'd been here weeks and still didn't know the musician. My desire to meet him returned.

I stood and stretched. "I think I'll go for a walk," I told Mom.

I had gone but a short distance when I realized the music was coming from Miss Sara's house. Confused, I walked toward the frame of light through the open doorway.

As I neared, I saw small figures huddled on the porch. Inside the house Miss Sara sat in her favorite chair, stringing tissue-paper flowers. Around her in a wide circle sat townswomen. They were making the colorful flowers while they laughed and talked. Tomorrow's decorations, I knew. But who was entertaining the children?

I moved to the gate, hoping to get a glimpse of whoever it was in the shadows.

Allen called out of the darkness, "Come in and join us. Come on. We've decided to sing. Haven't we, kids?"

"Yeah!" they cried.

"I don't think . . ." I stammered, too surprised to finish. Allen hadn't said he played a musical instrument when I told him about Jerry and his band.

"You don't need to be good. Just loud," Allen said, and struck the strings of the guitar. The children laughed.

I opened the gate and went inside the yard, grateful for the shadows that hid my face. How could anyone be this nice to kids and be a part of something evil? Ralph made room for me on the top step. Here nothing was as it seemed. The desert that looked so barren was filled with life. A boarded up mine held enough silver to make an entire town rich. And now Allen sat playing the guitar, and he hadn't even told me he could play.

"Do you know, 'Old McDonald Had a Farm'?" Allen asked.

"Sure."

He strummed a few notes. "Ready, kids?"

They sang the first stanza. Allen stopped. "Come on, April, join in."

"Okay," I said, and sang louder than anyone.

When we finished, Allen leaned forward. "Hey, you have a good voice."

"Not as good as I'd like. I wanted to sing with Jerry's band." I expected to feel sad remembering Jerry and the band and how far away they were, but felt nothing.

Allen interrupted my thoughts. "How about it, kids. Who wants to choose the next song?" From the many shouted titles he chose "How Much is That Doggie in the Window?"

I put my arm around Ralph, who had snuggled close as we sang. When we had finished, we chose another song and then another. I didn't try to analyze this new side of Allen. I was just glad for the now cooling breeze, the music and the good feeling inside me.

We sang until the women came out and gathered their children to go home. Everyone said how much they had enjoyed our singing.

"I hate to have it end," Allen told me. I was sorry, too, but didn't say so. He stood. "I'll walk you home."

"You don't have to."

"I want to." His voice sounded soft.

We strolled down the street bordered by an occasional lighted window. The wind was stronger. It tangled my hair and pressed my blouse close. Stars were scattered diamonds. "I've heard you play before," I said.

His hand found mine in the dark. "I'm glad you joined us. Tonight is the first we've sung since your grandfather died."

We went up my walk. "You play great. You could form your own band," I said, not wanting to talk about Grandpa.

"I don't want one."

He released my hand and opened the front door. "I wish you wouldn't ride tomorrow."

He sounded concerned, but I suspected the last remark was to change the subject. "Then I wouldn't be the winning rider."

He moved as if to kiss me. "Would you settle for being the prettiest?"

"Never." I laughed nervously. "See you." I slid inside and closed the door. I wished Allen didn't always make it so easy to like him.

"It was good to hear you singing," Mom called, as I passed her room.

"It was fun."

Next morning, Mom and I weren't the only early risers. Judging by the sounds coming from the street, everybody else in town was up. I looked out the front window. There were more horses and people than I'd ever seen there. Hearing their laughter and seeing the reunion of friends made me want to join them. My grandfather had mended the hurt and eased the pain of almost everybody out there. I pushed the thought aside. Tomorrow I'd think of Grandpa. Today I'd think of winning.

Mom came to the window. "I hope you or no one else gets hurt," she said. She turned away. "You'd better eat."

"I'm not hungry." For the first time in my life I was too nervous to eat.

I went out on the porch to get away from the smell of bacon. Allen waved and rode toward me on his stallion, still sweaty from his workout. I looked toward the Martinez ranch. The judges' stand was strung with tissue-paper flowers. "The race won't take place for hours," I told Allen. "Yet everybody is acting as though it will start any minute."

"It's a big day around here," he said. Somebody called to him. He jumped off and led his horse away.

I went back inside. Later, I saw Miss Sara on her porch and decided to ask her if I could string flowers somewhere.

Miss Sara wore a Western shirt, jeans and a cowboy hat. Seeing my T-shirt and shorts, she asked, "You haven't changed your mind about riding, have you?"

"No. It's too early to get dressed. Jeans and boots are hot." I felt my face flush. I'd just criticized the way she was dressed.

"You're right, they are. But today and Christmas are the two big events of Sand Canyon. I don't intend to miss a moment of today. Elmo always told me to dress like a rider makes you feel like one. I wish I were. I'd give them all a run for the cup."

"I'll bet with you riding him, Black Diamond would win," I said. I sat on the top step and locked my hands around my knees.

"Maybe not. I don't know the horse the way you do. By now you know what frightens him and if he has any strong dislikes, especially toward other horses."

I felt she was testing me, but I didn't mind. "I hope I do." But I wasn't sure I knew Black Diamond the way I should. After all, he was Larry's horse.

"I wish I could look into his eyes," Miss Sara said with a faraway look in her own. "Elmo used to say eyes reveal a horse's temperament. It's true of most animals, people as well."

"I should have been talking to you all along," I said.

"Maybe," she said. She talked of other races and of Elmo and how he said a thoroughbred can run up to forty-five miles an hour. I stayed listening, agreeing, until I knew I must eat and change.

On my way home Mrs. Garcia and Ralph called, "Good luck."

"Thanks," I said.

I had a bowl of soup and took my time dressing in a new red-plaid shirt and my old faded jeans and worn boots. I tied my hair back with a red scarf. My riding colors would be the color of the armband that held my post position. This I would draw at the race.

Mom and I drove out to the Martinezes' place early. Larry was already there. He had brought Black Diamond in a horse trailer hooked to the back of his car. If I'd thought the horses were restless earlier, these were twice as bad. Some were so lathered, they looked as though they'd been soaped for a shower.

The first thing Larry said when he reached me was, "Don't be nervous. You're sure to win."

I bit my lower lip and nodded. I tried to check out the horses that Black Diamond had to beat, but it was impossible to tell who was or wasn't in the race.

"Let him start easily, then tighten your hold smoothly and you'll get the most out of him," Larry reminded me. "And don't forget the other things I've told you."

"I won't," I said, unable to remember a single one. "But there're so many horses."

"Only sixteen to beat."

I grimaced. "Yeah, only."

"Last year's race had twenty entries. You'll do fine. You have last-minute jitters, that's all."

"I guess." Looking at all the horses I felt sure would get bunched, I knew anything could happen. I could be blocked, bumped, or in spite of the small warning flag on top, be pushed against the boulder. I shivered. "Why hasn't that been removed?" I asked Allen, when he rode up.

He glanced at the boulder, his expression grim. "It makes a good turning point and is added challenge. Try to keep out front. If you can't, drop back, but stay out of the pack. Winning isn't worth the risk of getting hurt."

"And where will you be?"

"I hope I don't have to be taking care of you," he said, and rode away.

I looked after him. Allen's not wanting me to race could be concern for me and not fear that I would beat him.

He had ridden in this race before. I wondered if he had won. I scanned the crowd. When I did, I saw Carl, the ranch hand Larry had fired that first day I'd gone to the Medford ranch to ride. Seeing Carl unnerved me. I hoped he wasn't in the race. He was sure to have a grudge against me. But until we had our sleeve bands showing who was in the race, it was impossible to tell.

We finally rode up to the judges' stand and drew a numbered sleeve band. I drew Number 3 post position. I'd have to get out in front fast or be caught in the mob. But I wasn't on the far outside the way Allen was; neither was I the inside horse.

We lined up, and somebody held up the gun. "You can do it," I whispered to Black Diamond, trying to settle him. I could understand his restlessness. I felt the way I did on top of a roller coaster just before it plunges downward.

The gun was fired. The horses bolted forward. I leaned forward, the stirrups carrying my weight. The horses crowded in. The stench of sweat mingled with dirt, and the noise of hooves and the screaming crowd enclosed me. No way could I get out in the lead. I searched for an opening. There was only choking dirt. Above the noise I heard Larry shouting, "Use the whip!" I gripped the crop but couldn't bring myself to use it. But I needed to get free. And I had no intention of dropping back the way Allen had told me.

Black Diamond moved up fast. Soon I'd be out of the pack. From the corner of my eye I saw a horse cutting across. I couldn't see the rider. His horse bumped Black Diamond. I tried to get out of his way. Then the boulder loomed up, huge and rough. There was nobody on my right. I was the inside horse. The horse on my left bumped again. The rider was trying to get me thrown. Fear froze me in position as my mind raced faster than the horses. If I didn't get away from the other rider, I'd be thrown and trampled, or smashed against jagged rock. "Get out of the way!" I screamed, my plea lost in the thunder of hooves.

Another second we would be in the turn. Swiftly and skillfully a horse and rider cut between me and the boulder. I recognized Allen. The one bumping me dropped back, and I saw an orange band, Number 10.

I turned for home, riding hard. In the fight to survive I'd lost ground. If I had used the crop, maybe I could have won. But I couldn't use it. I crossed the finish line in a cloud of cheers. The race was over.

Chapter Eleven

I held back on Black Diamond's reins, slowing him as others crossed the finish line, their own reins taut. Allen pulled up beside me. "You rode great. You almost won!"

Dust burned my throat and eyes. I was shaking. "Thanks for what you did back there."

"I saw an opening was all."

I knew better. "Thanks, anyway." I dismounted and began walking Black Diamond to cool him. The shaking inside me hadn't stopped.

Allen followed me. The crowd was gathering around the winning horse. "How could Mr. Martinez win?" I asked Allen. "I didn't even see his name on the list, didn't know he was riding."

"He was a late entry." Allen led his horse away, as

Larry pushed through the crowd, leaned down and let his lips brush my cheek. "Good riding."

"Not good enough."

Anger mixed with my fear. I searched the crowd for an orange sleeve band. "Number 10 bumped me. I could have really been hurt. Who wore that number?"

Larry removed Black Diamond's saddle. "April, everybody tries to bump a horse they think might win. It's part of the race."

"This guy was serious. He was trying to force me into the boulder." Just saying it made my mouth dry and my breathing quicken.

"Scare tactics. He would have moved away before you reached the boulder."

"Maybe," I said. I took off my scarf and wiped the perspiration from my face.

"Well, it's over. And you've won the second-place ribbon and a pouch of fifty 'lucky' silver dollars." Larry sounded pleased.

"Lucky because the prizewinner escapes with his life?" I asked ruefully. I was still scared and mad at the same time.

He laughed. "No, they're lucky because we're near the Nevada state line. Some winners have used the dollars in the casinos, and won." Larry handed Black Diamond's reins to a man he motioned to. "Let's go congratulate the winner."

Mr. Martinez stood flushed and smiling, but his eyes didn't smile when he looked at me.

"Anytime you want to sell him," Larry told Mr. Martinez, "I'm interested."

Mr. Martinez said nothing. A call came from the judges' stand for the three winners.

Allen appeared from nowhere. He snatched my hand. "That's us," he said, and led the way through the crowd. He'd come in third. I'd beaten him, but I felt no satisfaction in it.

"I'm glad you at least got third," I told him. "Maybe if it hadn't been for me..."

"You were bumped," he said, and lifted me to the judges' platform.

The crowd cheered louder. I smiled and waved automatically. But troubled thoughts distracted me. I needed to be alone with Allen to talk of that heart-stopping instant when someone had tried to drive me into the boulder.

One of the judges handed Mr. Martinez the trophy cup of silver dollars. He held it high for the crowd to see. I noticed that some sleeve bands had been returned to their places, and Number 10 was among them. I stared at it, feeling scared again.

Allen nudged me. A judge was offering me my ribbon and pouch of silver dollars. I quickly took them. He handed a ribbon and leather pouch to Allen.

Carl strode up to the stand and tossed the Number 14 sleeve band into the box. He grinned. "Good race."

I nodded. If Carl wasn't the one, who was it? I looked at the other riders. I could tell nothing by their faces.

I jumped down from the platform before Allen could help me. Mom hugged me. "I had no idea you could ride like that," she said. I didn't tell her I was riding for my life.

The crowd was already thinning, drifting toward Sand Canyon. Most were on horseback. Mom and Miss Sara rode back with the Garcias, leaving the Jeep for Allen and me. I got in on the passenger side and gave the keys to Allen. He drove in silence.

"You were right," I finally said. "The best horse doesn't win."

He glanced at me. "You did okay."

"I could have been killed. Who bumped me?"

"It looked like Carl on one of Medford's horses."

"It couldn't have been one of Mr. Medford's horses. He fired Carl. Anyway, Carl wore post position 14."

"Carl was working for him as late as yesterday. I saw him mending a fence."

The Jeep hit a rut, which tossed me against Allen. I righted myself at once, but the brief contact gave me a warm breathless feeling.

"Sure, Carl was mad because I rode Diamond," I said quickly. "But the rider who crowded me over wore Number 10."

"Carl could have turned in somebody else's number." Allen's knuckles went white on the steering wheel, then he released his grip. "Oh, well, it's over, and we're both winners." He eased the Jeep to a stop in front of my house and turned to me. "How about the dance tonight? Say I pick you up at seven?"

Surprised by his quick change of subject, I laughed. "If I go out on the porch, I'm there. Miss Sara said it's a street dance. Our entire street will be roped off. And our house is in the middle of the block."

"I know," he said. "I'll pick you up anyway. Okay?" His face was streaked with dirt, and his damp shirt clung to his chest, but I thought I'd never seen him look more gorgeous. I nodded.

Allen leaped out and swinging the small leather pouch, headed for home.

I sat wondering if Carl had mended one of Larry's fences and ridden one of his horses in the race. And if he'd tried to kill me. Allen might think whatever it was between Carl and me was as finished as the race, but I knew it wasn't.

I went into the house determined not to let Carl spoil the evening. As time for the dance grew closer, I washed and towel-dried my hair and poured perfume in my bathwater. Then I spread my clothes on the bed and tried some of them on. The new jeans and white peasant blouse I tried on last. I stood in front of the vanity mirror Mom had used when she was a teenager dressing for a date. I pushed my hair high atop my head and practiced provocative smiles, something I hadn't done since I was fifteen. Finally, my thoughts turned to the jeans. I'd worn jeans almost all the time I'd been in Sand Canyon. For the dance, I wanted to look pretty. I rummaged through the clothes on my bed until a pink cotton skirt caught my eye. I knew it was what I wanted to wear and slipped it on. It looked perfect with the blouse. I whirled around, my hair flying until I stopped and pinned it up. Stray curls fell loose at the nape of my neck and against my cheeks. My bangs were long, but they did give my eyes a mysterious depth. I slid the ruffle off my shoulders and studied the new April. Then I heard Allen's voice downstairs and quickly pulled the ruffle up again.

The minute I saw his face I knew I'd picked the right outfit. His cheeks were the color of his red-checkered shirt. Although his brown hair was neatly combed, a few lighter strands stood up in his crown as usual. They were something I'd always remember about Allen. He slid one hand in the back pocket of clean jeans and glanced at the toe of his polished boots. "You look great."

"Thanks." Allen actually seemed shy. That breathless feeling came over me again. The waiting room felt warm. "Shall we go?" I said, and opened the front door. Paper flowers circled ours and other porches, the wind making them rippling ribbons of color. Four men sat in the back of Mr. Martinez's truck, tuning their guitars and fiddles. Men roped off the area where the tables were.

Lights that had been strung earlier blinked on. Allen took a white paper flower from a post and pinned it in my hair. We went down the steps and into the street.

As we walked toward couples near the back of the truck, the music started, the warm night air carrying it to meet us. My fingers touched the ruffle of my blouse and slid it off my shoulders.

Couples began dancing. Allen and I joined them. I was surprised how easy it was to dance with him. Sometimes Allen held me close, sometimes apart, yet always our hands were touching. When he held me close, I felt his heart beat and thought of nothing but the moment.

Stars crowded the sky and moonlight softened the shadows. The street seemed filled with dancing people. Children danced, and their parents danced. Mom danced with Mr. Garcia while his wife stood by, smiling. I no longer thought of the race, but of the music and Allen.

Mr. Martinez started the square dancing, and I was thrown into a world of strange instructions. The speed was breathtaking. I caught such words as "Join hands, circle left, go around the ring. Allemande your corner, your partner right hand swing. Do-si-do and you promenade east. One and three lead to the right and circle round the track."

I was whirled. My hand snatched and released with speed. Others led me through the dance, laughing with me at my mistakes, which grew less frequent as we danced.

"Let's all get acquainted with a grand right and left. Ladies on the inside. Men on the out. Ladies to the right. Men to the left."

My outstretched hand was suddenly squeezed in a viselike hold. Surprised, I looked up into Carl's face. He wasn't smiling. He released his grip and was gone.

I kept moving by sheer will. I scanned the faces spinning past, trying to find Allen. Then I saw him. I wanted to go faster to reach him, but the music stopped. I stood before Larry, and let out my breath.

"I didn't see you dancing," I said, my voice carrying the relief I felt.

"I sure saw you." He smiled. His blue Western shirt matched his eyes. He looked happy and excited, as though he were having a good time.

"I think everybody did," I said, and laughed. "I've never square danced before."

The music started. We were partners. I was so glad it wasn't Carl, I said, "I'm sorry I couldn't win for you, Larry."

"Don't be. I'm satisfied."

"I should have used the whip as you told me to."

"It turned out fine. But I hope you'll keep riding Diamond, even though the race is over."

"Oh, I will."

The music stopped. "Promise?" Larry released me.

"I promise."

Allen came up, and Larry walked away without a word.

"What were you two talking about?" Allen asked.

"He asked me to keep riding Diamond."

Allen looked back at Larry. "I wish you were riding someplace else."

"Why? I love Diamond."

"What do you think of his owner?" Allen's voice showed no emotion. But the corner of his mouth twitched.

"He's okay."

Allen seemed jealous. What an exciting thought, but I doubted that it was true.

We went to the tables and filled two plates with food, then sat on Miss Sara's front steps to eat. I had seen her watching us dance earlier and wondered if she were reliving that long-ago Fourth of July. I knew, sitting there, listening to the music with Allen, that I'd never forget this one.

We finished eating, but neither of us moved. Apparently Allen felt as reluctant as I to break the special feeling between us.

Miss Sara came around the corner of the house, leaning heavily on a cane. She must have been coming from the cemetery. That was all that was back there. Allen and I ran to her. Seeing her pale and exhausted, I realized how much I'd miss her when I left at the end of August. We tried to get her inside, but she insisted on sitting in the porch chair.

"I'll make you tea." Allen's voice showed his concern.

She shook her head. "I'm out of sage tea." She looked at us, her face drawn in the moonlight. "Have you heard? Mr. Martinez has decided to sell his place."

"It's not his house he's selling," I said. "It's his horse. Mr. Medford offered to buy him earlier today."

"No. I talked to him. It's his land. He wouldn't say what changed his mind." All fight had gone out of her.

"Then the others will follow," Allen said in a hollow voice.

"Don't think of such things tonight," Miss Sara said. "You two run along and dance."

Allen bent and kissed her, then took my hand, and we left.

When he passed the dancers, I hung back. "I thought we were going to dance?"

"We are. But first I want to get some sage tea for Miss Sara."

The office was dark, but Mom had left a light in the waiting room. Allen hurried to the kitchen pantry. He filled a small paper bag with sage tea from a large bag on the top shelf.

Watching him, I remembered the night I'd seen him coming from the kitchen. "You knew right where to look," I said. "You've done this before."

His face flushed. "Lots of times. But I should have asked if it was okay. It was always okay with your grandfather. I just assumed..."

"It's still okay." I had to know for sure. "You can come in anytime."

"I did come in late one night, since you've been here. My aunt was having a hard time sleeping and I came to get some tea, then I told your mother about it later."

I had been wrong about Allen. I remembered how he'd followed me into the desert, and later to the Medford ranch. I had thought it was to spy on me. He had wanted to make sure I was safe. I'd thought he wanted me out of the race because I had the best horse. But he had ridden his horse between mine and the boulder to save me. And he didn't want Miss Sara to sell. If I was wrong in these things, maybe I was wrong in thinking he had anything to do with my grandfather's death. A weight lifted I hadn't been aware I'd carried.

I quickly turned to the stove. "Let's make the tea here." I decided Allen must never know I'd seen him that night or the suspicions I'd had about him.

When the tea was ready we hurried up the street, staying close to the buildings away from the crowd.

As we passed two empty houses, I saw Mr. Martinez standing between them. He was talking rapidly to someone I couldn't see. Whoever it was stayed in the shadows.

"Mr. Martinez is wasting no time in convincing others to sell." Allen's voice had a bitter edge.

"I wish there was a way Sand Canyon could remain just as it is," I said, and knew that I meant it.

"There isn't any way, with your grandfather gone and Mr. Martinez selling."

"Can't we do something?"

"I don't see how. They must have really scared him."

Remembering the way Carl looked when he had gripped my hand during the square dance, I shivered. "They? Who?"

"As I've said, I don't know. But I think your grandfather's death wasn't an accident."

"I know it wasn't. And we'll find a way to prove it. When we do, the people won't sell out."

Allen smiled. "When do we start?" His voice had the lightness of the square-dance caller.

"Now," I said.

I knew no more about what to do than I'd known about square dancing. I only knew we were going to try.

Chapter Twelve

I didn't see Carl the rest of the evening. When Allen and I weren't dancing or talking to those around us, we searched the crowd for Mr. Martinez. I expected him to come for his truck when the dance was over. But Allen said one of the musicians planned to drive it out to the ranch.

Looking about at the townspeople I wondered how many knew this could be their last Fourth of July race and street dance. By their rapid talk and quick laughter, I guessed most knew. Watching them hurt a lot, but it also made me mad at Mr. Martinez and whoever had talked him into selling.

Even before they played "Good Night, Sweetheart," and Allen held me close, I realized I'd grown to love this weird place and its people.

At my door Allen kissed me good-night. His lips sent

a shiver down my spine, and I wanted to cling to him. He moved away, a look of warmth on his face.

Later, lying in bed, I thought a lot about that kiss. Maybe I should have been thinking of how to keep others from selling their land and their interest in the mine. But Allen's kiss drove all else from my thoughts.

Next morning I wondered whether it was the magic of the evening or Allen that had made me feel romantic. I decided to take another look in the basement after breakfast, to keep my mind from straying back to him. It still seemed strange that an empty basement would be locked.

Wearing the red-checkered shirt and jeans of the night before, Allen arrived as I finished breakfast. He removed his hat, and the familiar strands of hair shot up. He must have known they would, because he tried to smooth them down.

"Want to come with me to Martinez's ranch?" he asked, sliding into the chair across the table from me. "Together we might get him to talk." His dark eyes never left my face.

My cheeks felt warm, but I didn't look away. "I plan to search the basement again."

I had to keep it casual between us. After all, I was leaving here at the end of August. But then, maybe the entire town would be leaving. The idea brought back thoughts of Grandpa and how he must have felt about it here. "Oh, well, I can always look in the basement later," I said.

"Great. Let's get going as soon as you're through eating."

"I'm through. But first let me check if Mom needs me in the office," I said. "We can use the Jeep."

"Good. Lately, when Martinez hears my bike, he disappears."

Mom didn't need me, nor did she ask questions. Maybe she was too upset by the thought of selling Grandpa's house and by having his beloved patients scattered.

I snatched up my hat and hurried out. Allen was waiting by the front door. When he opened it, it was like opening a furnace door. And it wasn't yet 9:00 a.m. Why would someone want this town? They could lease the mineral rights to the mine without buying the houses.

We drove toward Mr. Martinez's. "We'll ask and keep asking until he tells us why and to whom he's selling," I said.

"He won't. He's running scared."

"But you said—"

"I know what I said. But I could be getting you into danger."

I could see he was having second thoughts. "I've been in danger ever since I came here. And you must have known it. At least you knew that day in the street when I saw someone up on the mountain. You lost no time hurrying me into that vacant house."

"I didn't think you noticed."

"I noticed. Who do you think was up there?"

He shrugged. "I wish I knew. I was afraid it was the same person who took a shot at me from there. It was right after I found your grandfather."

"Why would anyone want to shoot you, Allen?"

"I think it was to scare me off."

"Whoever it was smokes cigars. I found one there."

"A half a dozen men here smoke them."

"Let's question them."

"You think the guilty one is going to say, 'Yes, that's my cigar. I did it.'"

I was getting annoyed with Allen. "Tell me their names. I'll question them myself."

"If you insist, start with Martinez. He smokes cigars."

"It couldn't be him. He was shot."

"He could have rigged up his gun and shot himself," Allen said.

"You think he would really do that?" I fell back against the car seat. "That's hard to believe!"

We drove into Mr. Martinez's yard in silence. The house looked deserted; an eerie quietness surrounded it. The row of trees stood motionless; there was not a breath of air to stir them. I stepped from the Jeep. There wasn't the slightest sound. I felt a tingling on the back of my neck, and my mouth went dry. If it were Mr. Martinez who had shot at Allen, we were an easy target.

Suddenly the front door flew open. Mrs. Martinez came out on the porch. "April! Allen! What a nice surprise. Come in." Although her voice sounded strained, no tension showed in her face.

Not knowing what to expect, I had stopped when the door opened. Now I hurried to catch up with Allen, who strode toward her, saying, "We came to talk to Mr. Martinez about your selling."

Allen was being up-front with her. If she didn't want this talk, she could say her husband wasn't home.

She stepped aside. "And he wants to talk to you, Allen."

As I passed her I saw new deep lines in her forehead and at the corners of her mouth.

The cooler made a whirring sound in the shadowed room. The few pieces of furniture were old and worn. Mr. Martinez slumped in a chair. He appeared so much a part of the room, the fear I'd felt earlier turned to pity.

"Sit. I'll get iced tea," Mrs. Martinez said, in that strained, falsely happy voice.

"Thank you," I said.

I didn't want tea. I sat waiting for Allen to start talking. I had thought that if he didn't ask questions, I would. Now I knew I'd never ask. Unless Mr. Martinez was a very good actor, he'd been forced to sell.

"Allen," Mr. Martinez began, "I need your help."

"And I need yours," Allen said, and I knew by the tone of his voice this wasn't easy for Allen.

Mr. Martinez straightened. "You're like another son. I'll do anything I can."

"Tell me then who's forcing you to sell?"

Mr. Martinez's face closed. "I can't do that. There could be accidents, killings. You've got to help me to get the others to sell, Allen."

Allen seemed stunned at the suggestion. Clearly he hadn't expected this. "I wouldn't if I could. I love this town. These people."

"So do I. That's why I'm asking you."

"Who shot you, Mr. Martinez?" I asked.

He looked at me. "Carl."

Allen leaned back. "Carl's a marksman. He wouldn't miss."

"He would if it was only to warn his victim. He's good at warning. He shot the hat right off my son's head, then laughed. Said his gun had gone off accidentally."

Disappointment turned my insides to lead. "The Carl who works for Mr. Medford?"

He gave me a wise glance. "Carl works for himself, and somebody back East. Larry Medford has nothing to gain by our selling."

"Carl tried to push me into the boulder during yesterday's race. Why?" Just thinking about it made my heart beat faster.

Mr. Martinez looked impatient. "He saw a chance to scare you. Thought you'd tell the doctor, and the two of you would get out of here fast. He likes to scare people."

"Then Carl was responsible for my grandfather's death." My words hung in the room along with the whirr of the cooler.

Mr. Martinez shook his head. "No. The desert got Dr. Joe. I kept telling him someday it would."

Mrs. Martinez hurried in, carrying a tray. "Iced tea, anyone?"

I took a cool amber glass and looked at Mr. Martinez.

I hoped the look said that I didn't believe him.

His gaze didn't waver. "I guess you'll be glad when school starts and you can see your friends. The desert is a hard place to live."

"It's been okay." I glanced at Allen. If the two of them were such good friends, why wasn't Allen trying to get him to talk?

"April, Allen. Do try my cookies. You two were so busy dancing last night, I don't think you ate a bite,"

Mrs. Martinez said. She chatted on about the dance and the horse race.

I finished my tea, then stood. Nothing could be gained by staying longer. "Allen, I've got to get back to the office."

"Sure thing." Allen scrambled to his feet.

Mr. Martinez followed us to the door. "Allen, think it over. You're disappointed in me for selling out. But it's for the best."

"I don't think so," Allen said. Only then did I realize how much his friend had hurt him.

"April..." The older man hesitated. "Your grandfather was the one first approached. So you be careful."

I nodded.

When we were in the Jeep and heading for Sand Canyon, I told Allen, "He was lying when he said the desert got Grandpa. But he meant for me to be careful."

"Yes. But remember, if he's scared enough to sell, he's scared enough to lie." I thought Allen was acting a little scared himself, but angry, too.

"Carl was the one on the mountain, and he also locked me in at the fort," I said, as the Jeep picked up speed.

Allen gripped the wheel, his expression one of rage. "We can be certain of that."

"Mr. Martinez as much as said Grandpa's house was the one wanted the most. I wonder why?"

Allen gave me a quick look. "Your mom won't sell, will she?"

"Not when I tell her what's going on here." Had it been just weeks since I'd wanted her to sell?

We rode in silence, my mind on Grandpa's house and the two rooms that had been locked. Mom's room was a shrine. The basement was empty. Remembering how frightened I'd been when Allen found me down there, my thoughts froze. And I remembered that just before he had pulled me from behind the bookcase, I had felt something cold, like metal, against my arm. Fear and anger blocked it out at the time.

The Jeep lurched to a stop in front of my house. "Let's go look in the basement," I said, trying to control my mounting excitement. "I think there's a wall safe down there and it's why Grandpa was the first approached."

Allen looked at me as though the morning had been too much for me. "There's nothing down there. We found that out. Your grandfather was the first one approached because he was a leader, and if he sold, others would follow."

He jumped out of the Jeep. "But if you want to look down there later, we can." He hurried toward home. Then he turned and came back. "Trust me. I would have heard about a safe."

I watched him walk away. Allen, you make it difficult to like you, I thought. I got out of the Jeep and went inside. The waiting room and Mom's office were empty. There was a note on the desk saying that she had gone to see a patient.

I had planned to wait for Allen, annoying as he was, but this opportunity to recheck the basement was too good to pass up. I hurried into the kitchen, aware of the hollow sound my sandals made on the wooden floor. A prickly feeling came to the back of my neck again. This signal of danger didn't stop me from opening the basement door. Taking a deep breath, I picked up one of the flashlights and clicked it on.

Darkness crowded the light, and rotting wood gave under my feet as I crept cautiously down the stairs. Intent on my fear, I forgot about the broken step until my foot caught on the piece of board. With a small cry I fell forward onto the hard dirt floor. The flashlight struck and went out, leaving only the square of pale light behind me. Groping for the flashlight, I fought for control. You're okay. There's nothing down here that can hurt you, I kept telling myself, until my hand closed over the flashlight and I turned it on again. But darkness had brought a feeling of being watched. By ghosts from the past? The light probing every inch of the wall only added to the eerie atmosphere.

At last the light came to rest on the bookcase. I moved closer and pointed the light into the narrow wedge between the bookcase and the wall. My body tensed. My throat went dry, and my heart picked up speed as the light traveled over rusty iron.

A door! An iron door.

I had hoped to find a small wall safe. Now I'd found a walk-in one. I put the flashlight down and tugged at the bookcase. My excitement made my work easier. In no time I had pulled the bookcase far enough away to examine the door. It was very old and had probably been here almost from the time the house was built.

Reaching out I closed my hand over the large rusty handle and pulled. And pulled again, this time harder. With a gulping sound the door opened. Snatching up the flashlight I shined it inside, then stared, confused. I wasn't staring into a safe but into a mine tunnel!

I took deep breaths, five, maybe ten. I kept thinking, I've found another way into the mine. Tell Allen. I raced up the steps and out into the street. There I slowed, not wanting to attract attention. Allen must be the first to know. He'd been so sure there was nothing in the basement.

I dashed up Miss Sara's steps and opened the door without knocking. "Allen," I called. "I found something."

"He isn't here," Miss Sara said from the chair. She stared at me with a puzzled frown. "Whatever you found certainly excited you. May I give him a message?"

I hesitated, wanting to tell him myself. "Just ask him to come to the basement at my house. Say I've found something. I'll explain later." I turned to leave.

"You found the iron door," Miss Sara said in a dull voice.

I whirled. "You knew about it?" Dumbfounded I came back and sat on the footstool to study her face. "I don't understand."

"I've known about the door since I was young. My mother told me. Alto Higg put it there when he owned the house. He was a recluse and afraid somebody would enter the house by the way of the tunnel."

"Then it leads to the main shaft." My heart leaped into a pounding dance. "Now you can prove there's silver. The others won't sell."

She shook her head. "They must not know. They must stay here. I'm close to Elmo. And one day I'll be buried beside him in the old cemetery. But for now, whatever I see brings memories of him."

I leaned forward, excited for her, and repeated, "You can stay. People will have proof of silver—"

She slumped. "Sam and the buyers were right, there's no silver. But I made everyone believe there is silver. I used some crude ore my father left me, and made sure people found it."

My rage climbing, I jumped to my feet. "These people could get killed believing in that mine. My grandfather..."

"I don't think your grandfather really believed there was silver. But he loved the town. In his speech he was to make on the twenty-ninth, I never knew if he planned to ask the people to sell or ask them to stay."

"Somebody thought it was to stay!" I cried, and ran. I had to get away from her before saying more. It's okay to have keepsakes from a lost love. But Miss Sara wanted an entire town as one.

But as I ran, a thought surfaced that slowed me. If there wasn't silver, what was in the mine and in this town to make somebody willing to kill for it?

Chapter Thirteen

I was almost to my front porch when I heard a familiar sound. Allen, on his dirt bike, sped up the road. I waved to him. While I waited, some earlier excitement returned, dulling the memory of my encounter with Miss Sara.

Allen, looking worried, pulled to a smooth stop and got off his bike. "Something wrong?"

"Come see what I found," I said. "An iron door." I tried to sound casual.

Allen came alive. "What iron door?"

"I'll show you." I snatched his hand, and we ran up the steps into the house. At the basement door I took a flashlight from the shelf. Allen grabbed the other, and we went down the stairs.

"Watch the broken step," he warned.

He needn't have. I'd learned my lesson.

"It's behind the bookcase." I shined my light into the opening.

Allen came up beside me and shone his light inside, too. "Maybe you've found another entrance to the mine. Good for you!" He hugged me. "Wait until we tell Aunt Sara."

"She already knows." I said.

He released me. "She knows?"

It was too dark to see his face, but I could hear the surprise in his voice.

"I told her when I went to get you." Now was no time to say more. Let Miss Sara tell Allen her secret. I looked into the mine tunnel. She could be wrong and there could be silver. Then Allen would never need to know the truth.

Allen moved closer. "Let's take a look."

In spite of my own eagerness, I drew back. "You think it's safe?"

The beam from his flashlight fell on wood shoring. He took my hand and said, "It looks safe."

With flashlights leading the way, we walked into the tunnel. It was like going into a walk-in grave. Almost at once we were encased in such darkness that our flashlights cut like laser beams. Stagnant air made it hard to breathe.

I took a step. Dirt and dust fell from the overhead shoring. I jumped back.

Allen whispered, "Don't worry. It's safe. Men used these tunnels for years."

"Tunnels?" I whispered back, wondering why people always whisper in them.

"Didn't you notice? We just passed another one."

"No. I can't see a thing. I wonder if this is such a good idea?" I remembered reading about some mining towns that had a network of tunnels under them, and shivered. What if we took the wrong passage?

Allen was close enough to feel my reaction. "Scared?"

"We could get lost in here."

"Not if we stay in the same tunnel."

"How can you be sure we're in the same one? In this darkness we could make a turn without knowing it."

"We haven't made any turns," he said.

I wasn't so sure of that. I wished we could go back, but Allen continued. I followed him.

"Watch out," he warned, and flashed his light on a small cave-in. We eased around it.

I scanned the lead-gray walls flecked with mica. "Do you think there's silver in here?"

"Not much from the look of the rocks." Allen sounded disappointed.

I walked along beside him in pitch darkness, hearing his breathing. Our footsteps echoed down the tunnel. I tripped on a broken board and dropped my light. A wave of panic caught me. "Allen!" I cried.

"Right here." He picked up my flashlight and handed it to me.

Although he had reacted quickly, my palms began to sweat and my heart raced faster. From then on I walked a little behind him. I was so close that when he suddenly stopped, I bumped into him. I stared with Allen at the solid rock in front of us. We had come to the end of the tunnel. "Let's get out of here," I whispered.

"Good idea. One of the tunnels is sure to lead to the main shaft. But we don't have enough light to search for it. I'll get Martinez and some of the others to come back with us."

We turned and started back. We eased around deep holes and mounds of dirt and rocks. It seemed forever since we had started. I swallowed and tasted dust. "I'm really thirsty," I said.

"We'll have the tallest glasses of water we can find when we get out."

"And we'll have lots of fresh air," I added.

His short laugh bounced off the wall and traveled down the hollow darkness. Allen seemed sure of our location. I relaxed. But not for long. We had stopped. I flashed my light on his face and saw Allen rubbing perspiration from his forehead with the back of his hand. "Darn!" he said.

His light, and now my own, rested on a cave-in that left only a hole at the top of the mine tunnel. It wasn't a fresh cave-in, even I could tell. "We didn't crawl through that," I said, and felt my body go hot then cold as I tried to push aside a sickening wave of fear.

Allen was silent. He knew as well as I that we were in trouble. Although I took deep breaths, I couldn't get enough air in my lungs. I kept thinking we were entombed.

Allen took my hand and squeezed it. He was trying to be brave when he said, "We'll be okay, don't worry."

We turned around. I could see the beam from Allen's flashlight, but couldn't see him. We walked in silence, each with his own fear. The walls seemed closer, the feeling of being closed in stronger. We tried another tunnel. Allen's light split the darkness. I pulled back. "We're going the wrong way," I said.

"No, we're headed right." How could he be sure? I wondered. Judging the tunnels was impossible; they all looked alike. I stopped.

"This has to be it." He sounded desperate.

I followed him, certain that he didn't know where we were going any more than I did. But I had no choice. I could only hope that he was right.

We had gone a short distance when the beams from our lights picked up a deep gaping hole cut in the tunnel floor. "Watch out!" Allen shouted, at the same time snatching me. We both fell backward as I heard the scatter of earth and the hollow sound of rocks falling. My light flew toward the rumbling where the floor had sunk even deeper. The hole was larger than I'd thought. I slumped against the wall, unable to control my shaking, too terrified to speak. No one knew we were in the mine; what would have happened to us had we fallen in?

"We'd have had trouble getting out of that," Allen said in a hushed voice that exposed his own fear. He tightened his hold on my hand and turned around.

I stumbled beside him, wondering which way we had come into the mine. Did we turn right or left? We must have been in here for hours.

As we left that tunnel, I stopped. "Wait. Let's mark this entrance so we don't go back in there again." I pushed three rocks into the middle of the opening.

I hoped Allen would deny we were walking in circles, but he didn't. I moved faster, his silent acceptance that we were lost adding to my terror.

"Slow down," he said. "There could be more holes like the one back there."

I stopped and flashed the light far ahead, seeing nothing below or above its beam. He released my hand. "If there's an air current—"

"I've got a match," I said, and struck it.

"No! Don't!" His hand snuffed the small, still flame.

At the same moment I remembered a chemistry lesson I'd had. "Oh, no! There could be gases!"

Allen let out his breath. "I know. But you just proved this tunnel is okay." He started walking again, slower. "Maybe we had better use only one flashlight from now on, to save batteries."

I clicked my own off at once. The strangling darkness was split by a single ray of light. Sometimes Allen allowed it to slide across the rough wall, but mostly it crept ahead to search out pitfalls or a familiar landmark. There were rocks, broken shoring and small holes, but nothing that we were sure we'd seen before. The feeling of being trapped grew as I walked. I held back a scream that tried to break free. I knew if I started screaming for help I might not stop. Gradually the tunnel became warmer, and there was a faint change in odors, or maybe lack of any. I wasn't sure which.

"I think we're near a flooded shaft," I whispered, and touched the wall to find out if it was damp. To my surprise it was hot. What did it mean? I jerked my hand away, turned and ran.

Allen caught me and held me close, then pushed my hair away from my face, saying, "Don't panic on me now. We'll soon get out of here and be heroes of the town." His words held a false hope that only frightened me the more.

After that, Allen kept slowing my pace as we stumbled along in silence. I knew it was to save my strength, and tried to cooperate. But the thought we might not get out kept spinning in my mind.

"This is it," Allen said. "I'm sure of it."

I followed him into another tunnel. Why had I ever shown him the iron door? If only I hadn't.

"There's a change in the air," Allen said. "We're near the basement or another opening." Now it was Allen who hurried.

I sniffed. He was right. I'd been so busy thinking about his being wrong I hadn't noticed the change. At the same time I saw the faint square of gray.

I heard the familiar snap of wood and a thud. Somebody had tripped on the broken step of the basement stairs. We had left the basement door open, and Mom, missing me, had come down to investigate. "Mom!" I called, beginning to run. "Are you okay?"

Silence.

"She must be hurt bad," I cried, then called, "Don't move, Mom. We'll be right there."

Allen caught me and whispered, "Wait."

As I tried to pull free, I got a whiff of cigar smoke. Someone was in the tunnel with us. Calling to my mother had not only told him I was here, but had also given him our location.

Allen clicked off his flashlight as another and stronger light entered the passageway. We ducked into a nearby opening. I tried not to breathe as the bright light traveled over the spot where we had stood a second before.

"Quiet," Allen whispered, putting his arm around me to draw me close. "Whoever it is didn't pick us up in his light."

"Who else could it be but Carl?" I whispered. "But how did he get in the house?"

"The front door is always open during the day."

We moved farther into the tunnel as the light came closer. My mouth was dry, and I couldn't stop trembling.

"When he passes, be ready to slip out and run for the basement," Allen said, his voice so low I had trouble hearing.

I tensed, ready to make a dash for freedom. Suddenly I was blinded by light. I stood frozen, waiting for a voice to come from behind the glare.

Silence.

"Who are you? What are you doing down here?" I cried, unable to stand the silence.

The light moved closer. I could hear labored breathing.

Allen snatched my hand again. "Run!" he said, and we dashed down the tunnel, followed by heavy footsteps. Earlier I'd been afraid of the dark. Now I welcomed it.

We moved into another tunnel. At least we must have, because the light passed us by.

I clamped my hand over my mouth to stifle the sound of my own breathing. My heart pounded so loudly I was certain the person behind the light must surely hear it.

"It's not Carl. I saw his outline." Allen sounded mystified. "This man is taller."

"Martinez?"

"Maybe."

We left the tunnel and groped toward the basement. But encased in darkness, it was impossible to tell if we were going in the right direction.

"Are you sure it wasn't Carl?" I whispered. "Carl shot Martinez and locked me in at the fort." Remembering the fort, I stopped. I had been afraid then, but nothing like now. I could hear our pursuer's hurried steps in another tunnel.

"Allen," I murmured, "how many cars does Larry Medford have?"

Allen took a moment to answer. He must have been thinking I had lost my head completely. "Just the Porsche. Why?"

"Medford didn't leave the house that day I was trapped in the fort. My Jeep was parked behind his car, and was still behind it when we left that evening."

I heard the intake of Allen's breath. "He would have been parked behind you when he got back. His driveway is circular."

"I know the car wasn't moved. I saw it from the tower earlier that day."

It could be Larry stalking us. I caught my breath, stunned. No. It could be Martinez or anybody out here. What was so valuable here?

The blast of light struck our backs and splintered, spreading to the wall of rock ahead. We had gone the wrong way. I spun and dashed toward the light and ducked into the first tunnel. I ran, stumbling, falling, getting to my feet to run again, knowing only that I had to get away from whoever was in pursuit. Somebody grabbed my arm. I cried out.

"Shhh," Allen whispered, pinning me against the rough wall. The light was nearing, swinging from right to left. Allen eased us into a niche. The light passed. I slid to the floor. Allen pulled me to my feet again. "We can't stop."

I staggered along beside him, gasping and using the wall as a brace. Because I was using my hand as a leaning guide, when we reached an opening, I fell into space. Groping frantically, trying to get to my feet, my hand closed over a rock, then found another close by, and another. The three I had put there as a warning not to reenter that tunnel.

A thought came. Maybe it would work. I couldn't run anymore. "Hurry," I said, tugging at Allen in one last spurt of energy. At the same time I clicked on my flashlight.

Allen grabbed to douse the light. "He'll see it."

"I want him to follow us." I swept the beam of light downward to the hole we had almost fallen into earlier.

"Good!" Allen caught on at once. "If I can get behind him when he comes in..."

"I'll make sure you can," I said, and eased along the wall toward the hole.

I sensed Allen grab for me, and was glad that he was too late to stop me. I had to get to the other side of the hole and keep our pursuer's attention. This was the only way I could think of doing it. Trying not to think of the gaping cavity inches from my feet, I edged my way a step at a time. Perspiration ran down my face, and my throat felt closed. My breath came in short rapid gasps.

Finally, I stood in the middle of the tunnel on the other side and shone my light toward Allen. He crouched near a shoring. For a moment I saw the relief on his face that I had made it across. Then I directed the light beam toward the tunnel entrance.

I waited, trembling. This might not work.

The footsteps picked up speed. A blinding light struck my eyes. My mind cried, Don't let him see Allen! Keep him occupied. "Please," I whimpered. "Tell us what it is you want of us?"

No answer. Just the awful labored breathing coming closer.

"Let us go. Mom will sell. And nobody will know about these tunnels." The light didn't leave my face. I coaxed it closer. "Who are you? What do you want? I promise not to tell anybody about this."

"I know you won't tell, April. Neither will Allen. Yes, I know he's in here with you." Larry Medford's voice held controlled rage.

Although I had thought it could be Larry, knowing that it was numbed me. I couldn't think or move.

The light lunged toward me. A terrified scream riddled the air along with the sound of tumbling rocks. Billows of dust turned the falling light into a pale orange glow.

I started coughing, and I could hear Allen coughing. Larry was coughing, too. We hadn't killed him.

"Allen, you all right?" I asked when I could speak.

"I'm okay. Fact is, I'm great! Hey, we're a good team. Let's get out of here."

"You can't just leave me." Larry sounded scared. "Bring help. Get me out!"

"Not until you answer some questions," Allen said.

"Starting with my grandfather," I said. "Why did you kill him?" The emotion of seeing the pyramid of rocks under the mesquite came back. I hated Larry now, as he stood in the glow of my flashlight.

"I didn't mean for him to die. I just wanted him to get lost so he wouldn't get back in time to speak at graduation. I was afraid he'd convince the people not to sell. I wanted the buyer to have time to convince them to sell."

"So you called for help and got Grandpa to leave his Jeep—" I started to cry.

"Your grandfather knew the desert. I expected him home the next day. I didn't know he had the flu. It wasn't my fault, I tell you." Larry sounded scared, desperate to get out.

"Why are some of the walls hot?" Allen asked.

"Hot!" Larry yelled. "Hurry, pull me out. This pit could fill with hot water anytime." He started clawing at the sides, making them crumble more.

"Then who wants the mine and why? Miss Sara told me there's no silver," I said.

"She told you that?" Allen sounded surprised.

"And she's right," Larry said. His face streaked with dirt, he glared up at us. "The shafts are filled with hot soda springs. A corporation back East wants to build a health resort where the town is, and to run pipes through these tunnels to each of the units for private hot springs." He paused for breath, then added, "Now help me out of here."

"Not so fast," I said. "How do Carl and Mr. Martinez fit in?"

"Martinez's dry lake bed makes a natural landing field. Carl thought he could scare your mother into selling."

"But you don't own land . . ." I began.

"Not here. On the mountain. It's just across the state line, in Nevada. The corporation plans to build a casino there with a tram from the hot-springs resort. That's if there is a resort. You kids help me. I'll see that you get good jobs at the casino when you're twenty-one."

Allen turned his beam of light from Larry to me. "Heard enough?" he asked.

"I've heard enough," I said, and started easing my way along the wall of the tunnel toward him.

"Hey! You're not just going to leave me here?" Larry sounded terrified.

"Maybe we'll send somebody back for you," Allen said. I said nothing.

I left my flashlight turned on and placed it at the tunnel's entrance. Then holding hands, we made our way back to the basement.

Allen stopped and turned to me. "You did it, April."

"We both did."

He put his arms around me. "Your grandfather would have been proud of you." He brushed a strand of hair away from my dirty face. "You two are so much alike."

"We are?"

"More than you know."

If Allen was right, then I knew a lot of things about Grandpa. I felt a warm closeness to him.

My thanks to Allen must have shone in my eyes, because his arm tightened, and he kissed me.

A flame burst free inside me. It touched every part of me. Allen released me and stepped back. I walked up the steps. This, my sixteenth summer, had been my very best summer ever.

Chapter Fourteen

Mom and I are back in Seattle. I'm busy with my senior year. Everybody at school tells me I have a great tan. Even Jerry. He wants us to date, but I make excuses. I wonder what I ever saw in him.

The Eastern corporation bought Sand Canyon. The people were willing to sell when they learned there was no silver. They also got more for the land and mine than Carl was offering.

Mr. and Mrs. Martinez moved to another state. But Miss Sara stayed close by. When the resort is finished, she is to return to a cottage there. She will tell true stories to guests of the history of the mine and Sand Canyon. The cemetery will remain, an agreement reached before Miss Sara would sell.

Mom is phasing out her practice here. We are going back next summer when the resort is completed, Mom as a doctor-in-residence. I plan to attend college with Allen in the fall. At least we can be together for a term before he graduates.

Maybe when Larry Medford gets out of prison he can still sell his land. But that's a long time away. And I don't think about it. Mostly I think of grades, Allen and what he said in his latest letter. I save them all. And I think of us being together next summer.

* * * * *

AVAILABLE NEXT MONTH FROM

Keepsake

A DARK HORSE

by Emily Hallin

When Wendy's dad runs for office,
Wendy meets a winner.

I heard a mellow voice behind my left shoulder. "Pardon me, but aren't you the candidate's daughter? The one who just spoke?"

"Guilty," I said, turning around to view an amazingly handsome face checking me out with melting brown eyes. Though I was too startled to take in the details, I got a general impression of tasteful elegance. A sweater of subdued color and well-creased slacks.

He put out his hand and grasped mine. "I'm Sterling Huffaker," he said. "I've been admiring you from afar. What a break for me that I had an errand in the bookstore, and got a chance to meet you in person, away from the crowds."

It was beyond belief that such a guy would be treating me like a celebrity. He kept his eyes on me with an expression of awe, and I knew how stars must feel when confronted by their fans....

Blushing Beauty—Do's and Don'ts

Avoid colors that are very different from your natural cheek color.

A defined line looks unnatural. Blend your rouge well so no one can see where color begins or ends.

Don't blush in a strip so wide that it covers your entire face. Blush is used to highlight cheekbones and add color to the face. Don't overdo.

Never apply blusher too close to the center of your face. Feel your face. Notice that the prominent part of your cheekbone starts around the area under the center of your eye, not at the bridge of your nose.

Practice with gels. A little squirt goes a long way.

Applying blush without a mirror is a mistake. Always watch what you're doing.

Don't apply blush before foundation. If you're wearing foundation, apply it first, blush second.

If you've tried applying a little blush as directed above but feel that you'd like to make a little more (or less) of your face shape, there are a few contouring tricks you can try with cheek color. Be sure to play and practice at home to see what works best for you. A few afternoons in front of the mirror will make you a makeup pro!

1. Think about the shape of your face. Is it square? Round? Rectangular? Triangular? Oval?
2. A hint for the round face: Put a dot of color on your chin and blend it in. This will help lengthen your face a bit.
3. Is your face long and narrow, like a rectangle? To soften the hard lines and widen your face, concentrate blush on the outer edges of your face. This will draw attention away from the length and give more width where you need it.
4. To minimize the hard lines of a square face, apply blusher normally, then dot a bit of extra color on your chin and the middle of your forehead. Blend well.
5. Triangular or heart-shaped face? Avoid putting blusher on your chin. It will only call attention to it.
6. Oval face? Anything goes. Try a hint of blush on earlobes, too, to give a fresh, country look—as if you've just come in from the great outdoors.

CROSSWINDS™

TELEPHONE OFFER

ONE PROOF OF PURCHASE

August 1988

Limited Quantities Available

ORDER FORM

Name ______________________________

Street Address ____________________ Apt. # ____

City ______________ State __________ ZIP ________

Orders must be postmarked no later than October 31, 1988. Incomplete orders will not be honored.

Send your check or money order for $5.00 with two proofs of purchase (one July, one August) and this order form to:

CROSSWINDS TELEPHONE OFFER
901 Fuhrmann Blvd.
P.O. Box 1396
Buffalo, N.Y. 14240-9954
U.S.A.

OFFER NOT VALID IN AUSTRALIA

POP-TEL-1UR